"You want a child, an heir. For Aldo," Giselle guessed. With every word Saul had uttered her own convictions and beliefs had become more and more revolted by what she was hearing.

The strength of those feelings overwhelmed her guilt and despair for herself. What Saul wanted to propose ran counter to everything she had believed about him.

Her voice was filled with angry passion and contempt as she told Saul furiously, "Even if I wanted to have a child, I would never agree to having one because you feel you owe it to Aldo. I would never sacrifice my child on the altar of your deathbed promise to your cousin—trapping him or her into such a set role even before they are conceived, never mind born. I won't agree, Saul."

Bestselling author

Penny Jordan

presents

**Power, privilege and passion
The worlds of big business
and royalty unite...**

The epic romance of Saul and Giselle
begins with...
THE RELUCTANT SURRENDER
On sale January 2011

And concludes with...
GISELLE'S CHOICE
On sale February 2011

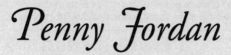

Penny Jordan

GISELLE'S CHOICE

The PARENTI DYNASTY

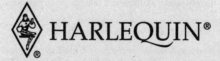

HARLEQUIN®

TORONTO • NEW YORK • LONDON
AMSTERDAM • PARIS • SYDNEY • HAMBURG
STOCKHOLM • ATHENS • TOKYO • MILAN • MADRID
PRAGUE • WARSAW • BUDAPEST • AUCKLAND

Recycling programs
for this product may
not exist in your area.

ISBN-13: 978-0-373-12969-0

GISELLE'S CHOICE

First North American Publication 2011·

All about the author...
Penny Jordan

PENNY JORDAN has been writing for more
than twenty-five years and has an outstanding
record: over 165 novels published including
the phenomenally successful *A Perfect Family,
To Love, Honor and Betray, The Perfect Sinner*
and *Power Play* which hit the *Sunday Times* and
New York Times bestseller lists. She says she
hopes to go on writing until she has passed the
200 mark, and maybe even the 250 mark.

Although Penny was born in Preston, Lancashire,
U.K., where she spent her childhood, she moved
to Cheshire as a teenager, and has continued to
live there. Following the death of her husband she
moved to the small traditional Cheshire market
town on which she based her Crighton books.

She lives with a hairy Birman cat, Posh, who assists
her with her writing. Posh sits on the newspapers
and magazines that Penny reads to provide her
with ideas she can adapt for her fictional books.

Penny is a member and supporter of both the
Romantic Novelists' Association and the Romance
Writers of America—two organizations dedicated
to providing support for both published and yet-to-
be-published authors.

CHAPTER ONE

HIS TOUCH SO SENSUALLY knowing and skilled, so male and powerfully demanding, sent excitement and desire spearing through her, leaping like wildfire from nerve ending to nerve ending, tightening the cord of longing he aroused in her until nothing else mattered other than his possession of her: swift and hot and *now*. It was always like this, his first single stroke of pleasure answering and inciting the desire for him within her that was as much a part of her as her breathing.

She'd known this would happen when she'd slid her naked body into the warm silky water of their private pool, with only the stars and the moon above them in the tropical night sky there to witness their erotic intimacy. She swam away from him, tormenting herself by her denial perhaps even more than she was tormenting him, and her gasp of hot sweet pleasure when he caught up with her, swimming with her and then under her, to suckle fiercely on her nipples, was accompanied by a shudder of wild pleasure. His hand slid between her legs, covering her sex as he kicked out, the strong movement of his body carrying them both through the water. Hunger and need pierced her in lava-hot waves that surged through her and set her body moving to the same rhythm as the caress of his fingers. She moaned softly, reaching for him, filled with the wildness that wanting him brought her.

They had reached the edge of the pool. Dizzy with desire, she let him lift her out and carry her to a wide poolside lounger with a mattress and towelling cover. He lay her there, her body soft and boneless, open to his gaze and his touch.

His gaze and then his hand stroked her naked body, cupping her breast. Her heart lurched into her ribs, the muscles in her stomach tightening with the same need that had brought her nipples into such an erect ache of eager longing. His gaze registered the sensual message of her taut nipples but his hand stroked on to cup her hipbone. Automatically her legs opened, the sweet wet heat of her desire pulsing through her. He bent his head, his thick, dark, still-wet hair sending droplets of cool water falling onto her desire-heated skin. His tongue-tip circled her navel, drawing deliberately delicate patterns against her flesh, drawing from her an agonised gasp of his name.

'Saul. My love. My only for ever love.'

She was possessed, engulfed, burning up in the need he had aroused.

He looked up at her and she gave a small helpless moan, her body arching up to his, to him, a sensual sacrifice.

She saw his chest lift and then fall, and then he was holding her, kissing her, entering her. She cried out her pleasure to him, wrapping herself around him, moving with him, until their bodies took hold of their desire and their pleasure, carrying them swiftly to the summit of their arousal and then beyond that summit to the shared freefall into release and satisfaction.

She'd closed her eyes, but now she opened them to find him smiling down at her, a possessive, tender, loving male smile.

'Happy anniversary, Mrs. Parenti,' he said softly.

Giselle smiled back at her husband, happiness filling her. She was so lucky. Their life together was perfect, the burden of guilt she had carried for so long a dragon slain by his fight to free her from it. There was no need in this moment of bliss and harmony for her to torment herself with the memory of that other truth she had withheld from him. It had no power over her now, no relevance in the wonderful life they shared—a life of fulfilling artistic ambition for her, working as she did as chief architect on Saul's worldwide luxury hotel developments, whilst the love they shared had created a private world of happiness for the two of them that neither needed nor wanted anyone else within its magic protective circle. They themselves were all they needed. Theirs was not a marriage that would ever include children. That had been the promise and the commitment they had made to one another when they had married twelve months ago. That was the foundation on which their marriage and with it her complete trust in Saul was built.

For both of them the causes of their determination to be childless lay in their own childhood and were understood and accepted by both of them. Just as Saul had healed so much of the pain of *her* childhood, with his love for her and his acceptance of her as she was, so Giselle had helped Saul to make his peace with *his* past—and more especially with the mother he believed had cared more for the orphans of the disasters of the world than she had for him.

It had been a very special and poignant moment for both of them when they had opened the first of what they planned to be a worldwide structure of teaching orphanages that incorporated both a home and a school in Saul's late mother's name.

Financed by Saul, designed by Giselle herself and built by Saul's company, the orphanages were to be Saul's gift of peace and acceptance to his late mother.

Their lovemaking the night after the official opening had been so emotionally and physically intense that the memory of it still brought tears to Giselle's eyes.

Theirs had not been an easy path to happiness and commitment. Both of them had fought hard against the fierce tide of desire for one another that had pulled them from their protected comfort zone into a combat zone in which they had both fought desperately against their feelings for one another, clinging to the wreckage of the security of their old beliefs. It had been Saul who had made the first move and reached out to her, and she, fathoms deep in love with him by that stage, had given in to her longing for him. After all, she had learned by then that Saul did not want children either.

As a billionaire businessman who thrived on the cut and thrust of competition, Saul had made a vow not to have children who, like him, would have to be left behind whilst he travelled the world. Unlike his cousin

Aldo, the ruler of the small European state their family had ruled for countless generations, Saul did not have to marry and produce a legitimate heir.

And so she had put aside the principles by which she had lived as an adult—namely that she would never allow herself to fall in love, because she did not want children and she did not want to deprive any man she might love of the right to have those children. She had already, after all, broken the first vow she had made to herself in loving Saul, and he had promised her that she was all and everything he wanted and needed. But even on their wedding day she had felt the shadow of her past chilling her happiness. Guilt was such a heavy burden to bear. A solitary and lonely burden too. Giselle shivered despite the velvet warmth of the tropical night.

Saul smiled at her, getting up off the lounger and picking up the bathrobe she had discarded earlier to wrap it tenderly around her. He must have noticed her small involuntary shiver and, so typical of him, moved to protect her. She always cherished these special moments in the aftermath of their lovemaking, and the last thing she wanted was for them to be overshadowed by the shadows of her past. Surely now fate had released her from the burden of her guilt? Surely now she did not need to remember that she was still held hostage to a part of her past about which Saul knew nothing? There was no need for her to exhume the raw and rotting corpse of her guilt. The cause of it did not matter any longer. She was safe—protected by Saul's love and by the life they shared that meant so much to them both.

'Hungry?' Saul asked.

Giselle looked up at him. He had the physique and the good looks of a Greek god, the courage of a Roman warrior, the mind of a master tactician allied to that of a Greek philosopher, and a social conscience that came from true altruism. She loved him with a passion and an intensity that filled her senses and her emotions. He was her world—a world he created and made safe with his love for her.

She nodded her head in answer to his question.

Their personal butler had arranged for a delicious supper to be delivered to their villa shortly after their arrival on this private tropical island that was home to a luxurious and exclusive development in which Saul had a financial interest, but then Giselle's appetite had been for her husband. They'd spent three days of the previous week apart, whilst Saul visited a new site he was thinking of buying and Giselle had gone to the Yorkshire Dales to spend some time with the great-aunt who had brought her up after the deaths of her parents and her baby brother. Three days without Saul had been three days and three nights too long.

Now, though, she was hungry for food, so she raised herself up on tiptoe to kiss Saul lovingly before he reached for his own discarded robe. The night air around them was languid with soft heat and the sounds of the tropics, and the fine gauzy layers of beige and black silk curtains they had to step through added a romantic intimacy to their suite. The decor of the villa was both modern and sensual, a palette of toning, layered off-whites and soft beiges and taupes, broken up here and there with the subtle use of pieces of black furniture.

Woven rugs in creams and off-whites softened the stark modernity of the granite floors.

A covered chilled trolley held their supper of hors d'oeuvres, mouthwateringly exotic salads, shellfish dishes and fresh fruit. A bottle of champagne rested in a bucket of ice.

'To us,' Saul toasted them after he had opened the champagne and filled their glasses.

'To us,' Giselle agreed, laughing and shaking her head in mock complaint when Saul put down his glass to hand feed her one of the elegantly arranged hors d'oeuvres.

Saul had the most beautifully male hands she had ever seen. Leonardo, she was sure, would have wanted to paint their image and Michelangelo to sculpt it. The familiar sight of their tanned sensual strength made her body tighten with pleasure.

He had fed her like this the first night of their honeymoon, teasing and tantalising her with tiny delicious morsels of food, until her hunger for them and for him had had her licking the savour of them from his fingers, just as he had later licked the juice of the fruit they had shared from her naked skin.

They had been married a year, and he could still excite and arouse her as swiftly and overwhelmingly as he had done when she had first known him. The fierce intensity of her desire was as fresh and consuming as it had been the first time he had made love to her, but now there was an added depth to their intimacy that came not just from their shared love but from her trust in him and her belief that he would always keep her safe. Safe enough to give herself to him without restraint, knowing that she could trust him utterly and completely.

'I want it always to be like this for us, Saul,' she told him passionately.

'It always will be,' Saul assured her. 'How could it not?'

Giselle shivered again, casting a glance toward the movement of the silk curtains as though half afraid of some unknown presence concealed by them. 'Don't tempt fate,' she begged him.

Saul laughed and teased her. 'I think it would be far more enjoyable to tempt *you* instead.'

They might already have made love, but their desire for one another was to Giselle like a pure clear spring of life-giving water, always there to fill and then refill the pitcher of their shared intimacy. It was the final few minutes she had spent with her great-aunt before leaving for London and the conversation they had exchanged then that was casting the unwanted shadow over her happiness now and making her feel vulnerable. She loved her great-aunt, and she knew that she loved her—just as she knew that her great-aunt's parting words to her had been meant to please her.

'It is wonderful to see you so happy, Giselle,' her great-aunt had said. 'There was a time when I worried that you would deny yourself the happiness of loving and being loved in return, and I can't tell you how much it means to me to see you so loved and so loving. I am proud of you, my dear, for all that you have had to overcome. When I asked you on your wedding day if you had told Saul everything I was so relieved, I can admit to you now, when you said that you had.'

Giselle had smiled and kissed her great-aunt but, like a thorn in soft flesh, her guilt had festered inside her as she drove home to London. It hadn't been necessary to tell Saul the 'everything' her great-aunt had referred to; there had been no point in releasing the private fear she had locked away. It wasn't relevant any more, and she'd been afraid of what Saul might think, of it changing things between them, stealing her happiness from her as it had done all those years ago.

She hadn't truly deceived Saul. He loved her as she was. And, secure in his love and his promise to her, she was never going to change. She would always be as she was now. She would always be safe.

'Come back. I hate it when you close down on me and go wherever it is that you won't let me go with you.'

Saul's soft words shocked her, prompting her to deny it immediately. 'I wasn't closing down on you, and there's nowhere I would want to go without you.'

Saul watched her. He loved her so much that the force of his love for her still sometimes stunned him and caught him off guard. Perhaps it was the intensity of that love that made him so acutely aware of even the most minor changes in her mood.

'You were thinking about your parents, your family,' he told her. 'I can always tell, because when you do your eyes change colour and darken to the intensity of those green malachite columns we saw in the royal palaces of St Petersburg.'

'My great-aunt said how happy she was for me

because I have you in my life,' Giselle told him truthfully, adding emotionally, 'I think I would die of the pain if I was ever to lose you. It would be more than I could bear.'

'You will never lose me,' Saul told her as he took her in his arms. 'There is no power on this earth that could come between us.'

They made love again in the deepest hours of the night, their lovemaking slow and sensual this time, a journey of a thousand deliberately lingered over and enjoyed individual caresses that made up their own encyclopaedia of very private pleasure. As they built step by step, touch on touch, the fire that consumed them both set them free from mortality for a few precious seconds of perfect unity.

Afterwards Giselle lay in Saul's arms, secure and at peace, floating in the mood of heightened euphoria that came with the aftermath of emotional and sexual fulfilment, falling asleep held safe within his love.

Saul was just drying himself off after his shower when his mobile rang, the sound causing him to frown. He had given his PA Moira instructions that he was not to be disturbed during this precious week he and Giselle had snatched from the busy needs of their lives other than in the most urgent and important of circumstances.

Giselle heard the ring of Saul's mobile from their bed, still warm from Saul's body and their early-morning relaxed and tender lovemaking. Through the voile curtains she could see sunshine dancing on the water of the infinity pool they had swum in the previous night. She could hear the rise and fall of Saul's voice from the adjoining dressing room, but was too relaxed and drowsy to concentrate on what he was saying—so it was a shock when he came into the bedroom, his hair still damp, a towel wrapped round his hips, with an expression on his face that had her stomach churning with the anticipation of bad news even before he told her.

'We've got to get back to London asap. There's been an accident. The full details aren't known yet, but it seems that Aldo and Natasha and her father have been the victims of an assassination attempt by one of Natasha's father's business rivals. There was a bomb in the car in which they were all traveling. Aldo had told me that they were going to England to look at a property Natasha's father wanted to buy there—a big country estate. Natasha and her father are dead, but Aldo is still alive. He's in hospital in Bristol. Moira's arranged for us to be picked up here by helicopter and taken to Barbados, where there'll be a private jet waiting for us. The helicopter should be here within the hour.'

Horrified, Giselle was already out of bed, going to Saul to hold him tightly as she told him, 'I'm so sorry— I'll get ready. It won't take me long.'

She knew how fond he was of his cousin, even though they lived such vastly different lives, and as she dressed and packed she prayed that Aldo would be all right. Poor Aldo. He was the most gentle and kind of men, and deserved a far more appreciative wife than Natasha. Giselle shivered, as she remembered what Saul had said. Aldo no longer had a wife. Natasha was dead.

She and Saul had just finished packing their cases when they heard the sound of a helicopter arriving. One of the golf-type buggies the complex supplied for its visitors to get around on was already waiting outside their villa. The breakfast they had been served when Saul had rung Reception to tell them that they were leaving remained untouched apart from the cup of coffee Giselle had poured for Saul—black and strong, his weakness and only addiction apart from her, as he was fond of saying.

During the flights from the complex to Barbados, and from there to Heathrow and then on again by helicopter to the hospital in Bristol—the nearest specialist hospital to the scene of the accident—Saul talked about his cousin and Giselle listened. She had met Aldo, of course. Giselle and Saul had first become lovers during a trip to Arezzio when she had accompanied Saul there as an architect seconded to his company by the practice he had been employing with regard to a new hotel complex.

Aldo was nothing like Saul. Where Saul was ruthlessly masculine and charismatically sexy, Aldo was self-effacing, an aesthete and a dreamer. Natasha, Aldo's Russian wife, had tried to convince Giselle that the reason Saul had sworn never to have children was because he resented the fact that his child could never inherit the role of Grand Duke of Arezzio. Saul, though, had made it plain that his reasons for wanting to remain childfree were based on his own childhood and the fact that his parents had been absent from it and from him, nothing else, and Giselle had seen that he was speaking the truth. Aldo loved the quiet backwater that was his small country, and had been grateful for the help that Saul had given him with its finances. A small price to pay, Saul had told Giselle, for the freedom he had to live his life the way he wished to live it because his father had been the younger and not the elder brother.

Giselle might not have liked Natasha but she would never have wished her dead—and especially not in such a dreadful manner.

The drips of information relayed to Saul whilst they travelled had told them only that because Aldo had been sitting in the front passenger seat of the chauffeur-driven car he had been spared the worst of the blast, but Natasha and her father had died at the scene of the accident.

'Natasha's father's business methods were murky, to say the very least,' Saul told Giselle. 'It's very clear that his deals have made him enemies, and many powerful people do not approve of what he's done whilst accumulating his fortune. And it's my fault that Aldo met Natasha.'

'Aldo married Natasha of his own free will,' said Giselle, trying to comfort him, reaching for his hand as their helicopter put down in a cleared area close to the hospital.

'And now she's dead. Aldo will be devastated. He adored her.'

A senior policeman was waiting to escort them to the hospital, answering Saul's anxious question about his cousin with a grim, 'He's alive, but badly injured. He's been asking for you.'

Saul nodded his head. 'And the incident?'

'We haven't spoken to him about it as yet. The fact

that the car was to some extent bullet-proof tells us something about Mr Petranovachov's lifestyle and his feelings about his personal safety—bullet-proof but unfortunately not bomb-proof.'

They had reached the hospital entrance now, and were quickly and discreetly whisked down corridors and eventually into an antiseptically clean and sparsely furnished waiting room adjacent to the private part of the hospital, where the Chief Inspector handed them over to a dark-suited consultant, accompanied by what Giselle guessed must be a senior-ranking nurse.

'My cousin?' Saul asked again.

'Conscious and eager to see you. But I should warn you that his injuries are extremely severe.'

Giselle looked anxiously at Saul, and said, 'If you want me to come with you…'

Saul shook his head. 'No. You stay here.'

'I'll have a hot drink sent in for you,' the consultant told Giselle, before turning to Saul. 'Staff Nurse Peters here will show you to your cousin's room. I'm afraid I can't allow you to have more than a few minutes with him. We've patched him up temporarily, but we need to sedate and stabilise him before we can operate and tidy up the mess made by the bomb.'

The mess made by the bomb. What exactly did that mean? Giselle worried once she was on her own. She hadn't liked Natasha, but her violent death had reawakened her own memories of the violent deaths of her mother and her baby brother, whom she had witnessed being hit by a lorry. For years she had carried the guilt of being alive when they had died, after sharp words from her mother had resulted in her holding back when she had started to cross the road with the pram. That holding back had saved her life—and filled it with guilt. Only Saul's love had enabled her to come to terms with the trauma of the accident.

Poor Natasha. No matter how selfish and unpleasant she had been, she had not deserved such a cruel fate.

In the hospital room Saul looked down at his cousin, wired up to machines that clicked and whirred, his head bandaged and his body still beneath the sheets.

'He's lost both legs,' the nurse had told Saul before she opened the door to the room, 'and there's some damage to his internal organs.'

'Is he…? Will he survive?' Saul had asked her.

'We shall do our best to ensure that he does,' she had answered crisply, but Saul had seen the truth and its reality in her eyes.

His vision blurred as he looked at Aldo. His cousin had always been so accommodating, so gentle and good.

'You're here. Knew you'd come. Been waiting.'

The words, though perfectly audible, were dragged out and slow. Aldo lifted his hand, and Saul took it between his own as he sat down next to the bed. Aldo's flesh felt cold and dry. The word *lifeless* sprang into Saul's mind but he pushed it away.

'Want you to promise me something.'

Saul gritted his teeth. If Aldo was going to ask him to look after Natasha in the event of his death then he was going to nod his head and agree, and not tell him that she was dead. Aldo adored his wife, even though in Saul's mind she was not worthy of that love.

'Anything,' he told Aldo, and meant it.

'Want you to promise that you will look after our country and its people for me, Saul. Want you to take my place as its ruler. Want you to promise that you will secure its future with an heir. Can't break the family chain. Duty must come first…'

Saul closed his eyes. Ruling the country was the last thing he wanted, and he had always felt confident that he would never have to do so. Aldo was younger than him, after all, and married. He had assumed that Aldo and Natasha would produce children to succeed to the title.

And as for Saul himself producing an heir… That was the last thing he wanted to do. He did not want children and neither did Giselle. For both of them what they had experienced during their own childhoods had left them determined not to have children of their own. That shared decision had forged a very strong bond between them—a bond that was all the stronger because they knew that other people would find it hard to understand. Only with one another had they been able to talk about the pain of their childhoods and the vulnerabilities that pain still caused them.

How could he discuss all of that now, though, when his cousin was dying and with his final breath asking him for his help—and his promise?

What was he to do? Refuse Aldo's dying plea?

Aldo had touched a nerve with his use of the word *duty*. Their family had ruled Arezzio in an unbroken line that went back over countless generations, but more important than that he owed a duty of care to this man lying here—his cousin, his flesh, his blood, who but for him would never have met Natasha. It was *his* fault that Aldo was lying here, dying in front of his eyes—because that *was* what was happening.

'Promise me. Promise me, Saul.' Aldo's voice strengthened, his hand tightening on Saul's as he tried to raise himself up.

'Waited for you to come. Can't go until you give me your promise. Must do my duty. Even though…' A grimace gripped his mouth. 'Hurts like hell.' Tears welled up in his eyes. 'Promise me, Saul.'

Saul hesitated. He could and would accept that it was his duty to provide their country with a strong leader, committed to doing his best for his people. He could give Aldo his promise that *he* would be that leader. When it came to the matter of providing an heir, though, Saul was a committed democrat who believed in elected rule. If he were to step into Aldo's shoes that would be the direction in which he took the country—leading it by example away from the rule of protective paternalism provided by centuries of his ancestors into the maturity of democracy. And with that democracy there would be no need for him to provide an heir.

Aldo knew his feelings on the subject of ancient privilege. But he was still asking him for a deathbed promise.

Saul looked at his cousin. He loved him dearly. What mattered most here? Being true to his beliefs and stating them? Or easing the passing of his cousin in the knowledge that in reality, no matter what Aldo was asking now, he knew what Saul's principles and beliefs were? Saul closed his eyes. He had never longed more to have Giselle at his side, with wise counsel and comfort to offer him. But she wasn't here, and he must make his decision alone.

'I promise,' he told Aldo. 'I promise that I will do my very best for our country and its people, Aldo.'

'Knew I could rely on you.' The grimace softened, to be replaced by something that was almost a smile.

'Natasha?' Aldo asked, speaking the word so slowly and painfully that it tore at Saul's heart. 'Already gone?'

Saul bowed his head.

'Thought so. Nothing to keep me here now.' Aldo closed his eyes, his breathing so calm and steady that initially Saul thought with a surge of hope that he might survive. But then he drew in a ragged breath and opened his eyes, fixing his gaze on Saul as he exhaled and then said quite clearly, in a wondering voice of delight and welcome, 'Natasha.'

Saul didn't need the flat line of the machine to tell him that Aldo had gone. He could feel it in the flaccid touch of his hand, feel it as clearly as though he had actually seen his spirit leave his body.

In the waiting room Giselle stood up when the door opened and Saul came in, knowing instantly what had happened, and going to Saul to take him in her arms and hold him tightly.

Neither of them spoke very much on the journey back

to London City Airport and from there to their town-house in London's luxurious and expensive Chelsea.

Once they were inside their house, an eighteenth-century mansion, Saul dropped the guard he had been maintaining whilst they had been in public and paced the floor of their elegant drawing room, his eyes red-rimmed with grief and shock.

'I'm so sorry,' Giselle told him, going to him and placing her hand on his arm, bringing a halt to his pacing. 'I know how much Aldo meant to you.'

'He was younger than me—my younger cousin—but more like a brother than a cousin to me in many ways. Especially after our parents died and we were one an-other's only blood relatives. I should have protected him better, Giselle.'

'How could you have?'

'I *knew* what Natasha's father was. I should have—'

'What? Forbidden Aldo from ever sharing a car with his father-in-law? You couldn't know that Natasha's father would be assassinated.' Giselle's voice softened. 'I do understand how you feel, though.' Of course she did. She had suffered dreadfully through the guilt and sense of responsibility she had felt after the deaths of her mother and baby brother. 'But you are not to blame, Saul—just like I wasn't to blame for what happened with my family.'

Saul placed his hand over Giselle's where it rested on his arm.

No one would be able to understand how he felt better than Giselle. He knew that. But the situation with Aldo was very different from her situation. She had been a six-year-old child. He was a man, and he had always known how vulnerable his gentle cousin was—to Natasha and all the pain he would suffer through loving her. But not this—not his death as an accident, a nothing, the fall-out from the actions of someone whose target was not Aldo himself.

'This should never have happened. Aldo had so much to give—especially to his country and its people.'

'He wanted greater democracy for them,' Giselle reminded Saul gently, not wanting to say outright at such a sensitive time that Aldo's death had opened the door to the country taking charge of its own future, electing a government rather than being ruled by a member of its royal family. Talking about the future of the country without Aldo was bound to be painful for Saul.

'I'm going to have to go to Russia—and the sooner the better,' Saul told her abruptly, and explained when she frowned, 'Distasteful though it is to have to speak of such matters, the fact remains that Aldo survived both Natasha and her father. Since the rule of law when there is more than one death in a family at the same time is that the youngest member of that family is deemed to have survived the longest, it means that by that Natasha, as her father's only child, will have inherited his assets at the moment of their deaths. And that in turn means that Aldo, as Natasha's husband, will have inherited those assets from her by virtue of the fact that he survived her.'

'Does that mean that as Aldo's only living relative those assets will now pass to you?' Giselle asked. 'I don't like the thought of that, Saul. Not just because of the circumstances of Aldo's death, and the fact that he has died so young. It's the nature of the assets, the way they were accumulated. I feel that they are...'

'Tainted?' Saul suggested, and Giselle nodded her head. 'I share your feelings, and certainly the last thing I want or intend to allow to happen is for me to have any personal benefit from that money. However, I have a duty to Aldo and to the country—to do what is right for them. It was thanks to Ivan Petranovachov's bad advice that Aldo invested so heavily and unwisely in ventures that led to him losing a great deal of money. I know that I helped him out by clearing his personal debts, but the country itself is still heavily burdened with loans that Aldo took out, intending to use the money for the benefit of his people. Unfortunately most of that money ended up in schemes that benefited those who proposed them—many of them business associates of Natasha's father.'

Giselle nodded. None of this was new to her. She was well aware of how angry Saul had been when Natasha had announced so smugly just after Christmas, when they had visited them, that she had insisted on Aldo ignoring Saul's advice and turning to her own father instead. Aldo, sweet-natured though he had been, had not had a very good head for business.

'What I plan to do first of all is speak to Natasha's father's Russian partners and business associates and find out exactly what the situation is. Then I'll set about selling off the assets and using that money to clear Arezzio's outstanding debts brought about by Aldo's ill-advised investment of the country's money in Ivan Petranovachov's business enterprises. Anything that is left I intend to give to charity. Not our own charity. I don't want that tainted by money wrung out of businesses that rely on cheap enforced labour—which is what I suspect many of Ivan Petranovachov's businesses do. I shall speak to someone in authority at the Russian Embassy and ask them to recommend suitable recipients for the money.'

'I think that's an excellent idea,' Giselle approved. 'When will we need to leave for Russia?'

Saul shook his head. 'I don't want you to come with me, Giselle.'

She tried to hide how much his statement upset her, but it was impossible for her to conceal her feelings. 'We always try to travel together, and especially on an occasion like this, I want to be with you.'

To give him her support. Saul knew that was what she meant.

'I know,' he agreed, 'and believe me there is nothing I want more than to have you with me, supporting me.' He gave her a tender smile. 'We work so well together. It's thanks to you that we founded our orphanage charity, and that, as you know, has done so much to help me lay the anger and negativity I felt towards my mother to rest. But I doubt I'll be well received by some of Ivan Petranovachov's business colleagues. I don't want you being subjected to any unpleasantness—or danger.'

Giselle's heart thudded against her breastbone. 'And I don't want *you* to be in danger.'

'I shall be very careful,' he assured her. 'But it will be easier for me to do what has to be done if I don't have to worry about your safety. I won't be gone long. Three or four days at the most.'

Giselle exhaled unhappily. What Saul was saying made sense, but they'd only just spent some time apart. However, she didn't want to add to the burdens that Saul was already carrying at such a tragic and unhappy time by making a fuss and having him worry about her, as well as dealing with the complications caused by Aldo's death.

'I understand,' she told him, unable to resist adding ruefully, despite her good intentions, 'I just hate us being apart so much. You'll have to blame yourself for that, for making me so happy.'

Saul smiled down at her. 'That's a two-way street, you know. You make me happier than I ever imagined I could be, and that only makes me feel even more guilty about Aldo. We both know that his marriage can't have brought him anything like the happiness *we* share. There was never any real emotional commitment or closeness between him and Natasha.'

'He loved Natasha but I don't think she loved him in the same way.'

'Our relationship is built on mutual honesty and trust. I know you would never conceal anything from me. I doubt very much that Aldo could ever have said that about Natasha.'

Giselle rested her head on Saul's shoulder, her heart thumping with the guilt that thudded through her. She *had* kept something concealed from Saul. But it was nothing he needed to know, nothing that affected her love for him. In fact, if anything, what she hadn't told him only made her love for him stronger and deeper, because their shared decision not to have children meant that what she hadn't told him need not matter.

'I love you so much,' she told him now. 'Our life together is everything I hoped it would be and more.'

'I agree. You are the best, Giselle. You bring out the best in me. You are my love and my life.' Saul drew her closer and kissed her, tenderly at first and then more hungrily. Life was so precious, and so was love, and the need to drive away the darkness of Aldo's death and find comfort and solace in the act of love surged through him.

Giselle responded immediately, returning his kiss with her own desire. Sometimes actions and emotions did not need words or explanation.

Saul left for Russia the next day, after an early morning appointment at the Russian Embassy to discuss his plans and get approval for them. He had reassured himself that Giselle, who had woken in the night feeling unwell— the result of their rushed flight back to the UK and the shock of the assassination, they both agreed—was back to her normal self, even if her stomach did still feel rather delicate.

Their own affairs would have to be put on hold for now, Giselle knew. There would be Aldo's funeral to arrange—a state funeral, of course, given his position. Natasha was to be buried with him, but the Russian Embassy had undertaken to arrange her father's funeral.

Giselle decided to spend the time whilst Saul was

away working on her plans for the island Saul had bought, the acquisition of which had originally brought them together. Saul had given the island to her as a surprise wedding gift, and they had decided that instead of building a luxurious hotel complex on it, as had been Saul's original plan, the island would become home to a holiday complex for orphaned and deprived children. Giselle was in negotiations with various theme parks with a view to creating something very special indeed for those children.

Just one of the things that had deepened her love for Saul was the fact that he understood her need for their charitable work to be focused on children because of the death of her baby brother. She knew, of course, that nothing could bring her brother back to life, just as nothing could ever completely take away the guilt that she suffered, but she still felt driven to do something to help children whose lives she could do *something* to save.

Because of her baby brother…*and because of the children she could never have?*

Giselle pushed away the plans on which she had been working in the light-filled studio—Saul had turned the house over to her after their marriage, for her to reorganise as she wished, and the large double office and workspace she had created out of the original darkly formal and masculine library had delighted him as much as it did her.

The children she could never have for their own sake, for their *safety* when they were small and vulnerable, and for their ability to live their lives without the fear that had stalked her life once they were adult.

Had stalked hers? Was she *sure* that that fear was truly in the past? Of course she was. Saul had given her his love and his assurance that he did not want children, and her husband was above all else a man of his word. A man she could trust.

Giselle stood up, blinking away the sudden rush of tears that clouded her vision. Why was she crying when she had so much? When she had Saul's love? When it was in part their shared determination not to have children that had bonded them together? Did she really need to ask herself that? Every time they visited the children supported by their charity, when she spoke to or held one of them, it made her ache to hold Saul's child, but that could and must never be.

Her mobile rang. She looked at it, smiling when she saw that her caller was Saul.

'It's just a quick call,' he told her. 'Just to make sure you're all right.'

'I'm fine—what about you?' she asked anxiously.

'I'm getting through things, so it shouldn't be too long before I'm back.'

'I miss you,' Giselle told him.

'I miss you, too,' was his answer.

After their call had ended Giselle promised herself that once all the formalities to do with Aldo's death were over she'd suggest to Saul that they took a few days out together—not just to make up for the time they had lost in rushing back to England, but also so that Saul could mourn Aldo privately.

* * *

In Moscow Saul stared out of his hotel bedroom window. The deathbed promise Aldo had demanded from him still weighed heavily on him. Ruling Arezzio had always been the last thing he had wanted to do, and he had been glad that it was Aldo who had inherited that responsibility and not him. He loved the life he and Giselle had built for themselves, and he knew that Giselle did too. Just as the loss of their parents and their childhoods had left them both with the belief that they hadn't mattered, that they had not been loved by their parents, had bonded them together, so had their shared enjoyment of their business activities. Their lives during the year of their marriage had focused on their love for one another and their duty to that love.

Now, though, he had another duty to consider. A duty that would totally change the way he and Giselle lived their lives and which would impose on them all the demands that came with taking on the mantle of hereditary ruler—the next in a long line of such rulers, father and son, over centuries of generations.

He would be glad to leave Russia—and not just because he missed Giselle. The behaviour of Natasha's father and some of his business associates had left a bad taste in his mouth, and he had seen from his meetings with the relevant Russian officials that they shared his distaste for the manner in which Ivan Petranovachov had accumulated his vast fortune.

Around Natasha's neck at the time of her death had been a necklace which Saul had been informed had belonged to the last Tsarina—a piece of such historic value that its rightful home was a museum. And yet somehow

Natasha's father had been able to gain possession of this piece. Saul had been glad to hand it over to the Russian authorities, tainted as it was by the fate of the Tsarina for whom it had been designed. He smiled to himself, knowing what Giselle's reaction would be were he to tell her that he wished to commission a piece of jewellery for her worth a king's ransom. She would immediately insist that he put the money into their charity instead.

Giselle. Saul felt an urgent need to be with her, holding her, feeling the living warmth of her in his arms as they made love.

CHAPTER TWO

THE SIGNS OF MOURNING grew as they drove towards the capital city of Arezzio: black flags bearing Aldo's crest at half-mast on every lamppost, as well as hanging from the windows of so many of his people. It brought a lump of emotion to Giselle's throat. She turned to Saul to tell him so, and then stopped.

Saul was not looking at her. He was looking away from her. She had known that Saul would be affected by his cousin's death, but since he had returned from Russia at the beginning of the week, after their initial fierce and joyous reunion lovemaking, Saul had seemed to retreat from her into his own thoughts. At first she had put it down to his natural grief, but now she was beginning to feel that Saul was deliberately excluding her from his thoughts and feelings about the loss of his cousin. Whenever she tried to talk to him about Aldo he cut her off and changed the subject, as though he didn't want to share what he was feeling with her. Why? Didn't he understand that his refusal to talk about Aldo to her was making her feel shut out and rejected?

She reached for his hand, her movement causing him to turn and look at her.

'Something's wrong,' he guessed. 'What is it?'

Relief filled her, and with it gratitude for Saul's perceptive awareness.

'You've seemed so guarded and withdrawn since you got back from Russia, I was beginning to worry.'

'I'm sorry. I've been struggling to come to terms with what Aldo's death is going to mean. It never crossed my mind that he might die so young, or to consider how that might impact on the future of the country.'

'Aldo's people will miss him,' she said quietly. 'I know that neither of us really approved of the way the country was run, with Natasha having such a strong influence on Aldo and when we both feel so strongly about democracy, but Aldo tried his best to be a good ruler. Natasha liked to complain that he put the country first, before her.'

'That wasn't true, of course, but Aldo did try his best to do his duty. It wasn't his fault that Natasha was so determined to have her own way. Also, he believed sincerely in the right of the people to *expect* him to put his duty to them before everything else—just as he believed in the importance of the tradition of that duty being passed down through the generations.'

'Your strong sense of duty and loyalty to those you care about is something you and Aldo share…shared,' Giselle amended quickly, relieved when Saul squeezed her hand rather than looking upset because she had referred to Aldo in the present tense.

She felt much better now that they were talking about Aldo, about Saul's feelings. Her childhood had left her with a fear of being excluded from the emotions of those she loved, and she suspected that it sometimes made her over-sensitive on that issue.

They had reached the palace now, where the Royal Guard was on duty, their normal richly coloured uniforms exchanged for mourning black, their tunics, like the flags, embroidered in scarlet and gold with the royal house's coat of arms.

Tradition, like pomp and ceremony, could have a strong pull on the senses Giselle recognised as they were met from the car by one of Aldo's elderly ministers, who bowed to Saul and then escorted them up the black carpet and into the palace. She tended to forget that Saul carried the same royal blood in his veins as his cousin—principally because Saul himself had always made it so clear to her that he had distanced himself from the whole royalty thing.

Saul had his own apartment within the palace, and Giselle was relieved that he had it, so that they could retreat to it after the ritual and ceremony of the public declaration of mourning that naturally dominated the atmosphere. Even the maids were dressed in black, and all the household staff looked genuinely upset by the loss of a ruler Giselle knew had been much loved, despite the fact that his gentle nature had made it next to impossible for him to stand up to both his wife *and* those who had wanted to use Arezzio for their own profit via a series of schemes that Giselle knew Saul had tried to dissuade Aldo from adopting.

'Things will be very different here now for the people,' she commented when she and Saul were finally alone in his apartment.

'Yes,' Saul agreed.

He felt relieved that, even though she had not said so directly, Giselle's comments about the future of the country meant she was aware of the role he would have to take. He was grateful to her for not insisting on discussing it, and so giving him the space he felt he needed to come to terms with what lay ahead.

When he had given his promise to Aldo his behaviour had been instinctive and emotional. It had only been afterwards that he had truly recognised what that promise meant. Then he had balked at the burden Aldo had deliberately placed on him. He had even felt resentful and angry with his cousin, since Aldo had *known* that he had always been glad that his father had been the younger brother and he would not inherit either the title or its responsibilities. Those feelings had tormented him whilst he had been in Russia, and he had longed for Giselle to be there so that he could unburden himself to her.

Coming back here today, he felt that sense against hostility to the burden Aldo had placed on him burn very strongly in him. The weight of his responsibility to his cousin and to their royal blood weighed as heavily on him as the mourning that clothed the palace and its inhabitants.

Now, just by walking into his own apartment with Giselle, he could feel that burden lifting, the pressure of the decision he knew he had to make easing. Giselle's calm and wise words about his inborn sense of duty had helped to guide him in the right direction.

'The changes that will have to be made will benefit

the people—even if right now they might not be able
to see that,' said Giselle. "We all loved Aldo, but the
reality is that the country needs a strong and motivated
leadership. Perhaps his death was fate's way of saying
that it is time for things to change.'

Saul was even more convinced that she had realised
the impact Aldo's death must have on their own lives.
The knowledge comforted and strengthened him.

'Have I told you how much I love you?' he asked.

Giselle smiled at him in relief. He had seemed so
preoccupied and distant, but now she could see that he
was her beloved Saul again.

'It was here that we first made love.' He smiled at
her and slid his hand beneath the soft weight of her hair
to draw her closer to him. Giselle smiled back at him,
but their movement towards one another was halted by
a firm knock on the door.

Releasing her, Saul went to answer it. Giselle could
see the black-garbed major-domo standing outside in
the corridor, and Saul was inclining his head towards
him to hear what he was saying, before nodding and
then closing the door to come back to her. The warm
intimacy had been stripped from his expression, and in
its place was a shuttered grimness.

'Aldo's body will be lying in state in the cathedral
from tomorrow morning. The major-domo says that I
may pay my last respects privately now if I wish.'

'I'll come with you—' Giselle began, but Saul shook
his head.

'No. I... It's best if I go alone. You and I will be

expected to open the official lying in state tomorrow. We can go together then.'

He had gone before Giselle could make any further objections. The door closed behind him with a sharp click, like an axe falling between them and separating them, Giselle thought uneasily.

There was a private underground passage that led from the palace to the cathedral, hewn out of the rock on which the city was built. The tunnel might now be illuminated by electric lights, but as he followed the major-domo Saul admitted that it wasn't hard to imagine it lit only by torches as those using it moved down it with a potentially more dangerous and even sinister purpose at a time when the country had been besieged by its enemies and those who coveted it.

The country had broken away from the Catholic church at the same time as Britain's Reformation, and now its religion could best be described as Protestant high church.

The Archbishop was waiting to receive him, his formal robes a touch of bright shimmering colour after the darkness of the tunnel and the mourning-shrouded castle.

The cathedral reminded Saul of a smaller version of Westminster Abbey. Above the high altar was a stained glass window, depicting the brave deeds of his ancestors before they ascended to heaven escorted by winged archangels.

Aldo's white-silk lined coffin was in the centre of the cathedral. Aldo himself was dressed in the ceremonial robes of rulership. The smell of incense hung on the air like the words of prayer the Archbishop murmured before he and the major-domo retreated to leave Saul alone with his cousin.

In death, Aldo's features had gained a stark dignity that made him look more severe than he had been. Such a gentle man, who had not deserved the cruelty of his fate. A man to whom Saul had given his word, his promise, that he would take up the yoke of rulership that Aldo had been forced to cast down.

Silently Saul knelt beside Aldo's coffin. It was too late for him to change his mind. He had given his word. With that acceptance came a sense of relief and release, a lightening of the grim mood of resentment that had been gripping him.

Giselle had been right when she had said the country needed a strong ruler. There was so much that such a ruler could do for his people. He could provide them with the schools needed to give them a better education. He could make money available for them to study at the world's best universities and then bring what they had learned back to their country. He could in time endow their own university, where those people could pass on to others their knowledge. He could turn his country from inertia and poverty into a powerhouse of creative energy. It was a project he knew would appeal to Giselle.

He could be the ruler Aldo had wanted him to be, the ruler he had promised he would be, but to do so he would have to turn his back on the life he and Giselle had created together. They would have to sacrifice its freedoms of choice for the onerous burdens of state and expectation, of tradition and ceremony.

Saul stood up.

The first thing Saul did when he got back to his apartments was take Giselle in his arms and hold her tightly.

He smelled of cold air and incense, Giselle recognized, and she felt his chest expand under the deep breath he took before he exhaled heavily.

She lifted her face to look at him, but he shook his head and then kissed her, a fiercely passionate and demanding kiss of such intensity that Giselle's own emotions immediately responded to it.

He couldn't trust himself to talk to Giselle about Aldo's death, Saul recognised. The pain he felt at losing his cousin so unexpectedly and so shockingly held unwanted echoes of the despair and anger he had felt at the deaths of his parents, and with it came an awareness of his own vulnerability through those who mattered to him. If there was one thing Saul found hard to handle it was the thought of being emotionally vulnerable.

It was easier to act than to speak—easier to lose himself in a physical expression of the need he felt for Giselle's proximity, for the comfort of her living, breathing presence. Easier to hold her and love her than to tell her how he felt. A man did not show his weakness, after all—not even to the woman he loved. Because she surely needed him to be strong for both of them.

It was like being new lovers again, or lovers who had been parted for too long, Giselle thought. Saul's hunger for her was that of a man who had suppressed a need he could no longer control. It was arousing her and disarming her too, making her feel that nothing mattered other than their love. The sympathy she had wanted to show him, the comfort she'd wanted to give him, was expressed best via their physical commitment to one another. There was a wildness, a fierceness, almost a savagery about the way he touched her, groaning his pleasure against her mouth when he cupped her breast. His desire ignited her own, so that the silence of the room quickly became broken by the sounds of their need, the harsh gasped breaths, the rasp of hands on fabric, the moan of triumph or despair when a new intimacy was gained or denied by the barrier of clothes that their growing passion not only wanted but needed to cast aside.

This was not the lovemaking of a gentle, accommodating lover. This was the mating of a man's most basic predatory sensual need, and a woman's—*his* woman's—hunger to meet that need, Giselle recognized, as Saul bared her breasts to his gaze and then his touch with a raw sound of triumph.

His hands on her flesh, his fingertips stroking, shaping and then erotically tugging on the flaunting arousal of her nipples, made her shudder convulsively in wanton pleasure. This was their desire for one another stripped bare to its most raw and sensual elements. This was need brought to a pure boiling point of intensity that was just this side of dangerous and starkly shocking.

A woman would have to trust a man completely to give herself over to such a consuming conflagration of desire. And she did, Giselle acknowledged, as she felt its heat burning inside her just as the heat of Saul's touch burned her flesh.

'Kiss me,' she commanded him, knowing that she was walking into the heart of the fire, giving herself over to it and to him to do as he wished.

They were no strangers to the intensity of their own passion, their hunger for one another, but now there was another element to their lovemaking—or so it seemed to Giselle. As though death had honed and sharpened Saul's appetite for life, and for her. There was an urgency, a need, a driven and heightened edge to their intimacy as Saul anointed and worshipped every sensual part and threshold of her body until he had tightened the sharp spirals of her desire to the point where she could bear it no longer, and she had to beg him to end her torment, to fill the aching, longing emptiness within her.

Her initial climax was sharp and immediate, but Saul drove them both on with deep passion-filled strokes within her that took her beyond her own experience to a place where her flesh clung to his for support during their shared journey just as she clung to him.

The cry that Saul uttered in the final seconds of their shared release seemed to Giselle to be wrested from the very heart of him.

Lying holding Giselle, whilst his heartbeat slowed back to its normal rate, Saul felt his own relief fill him. They were alive, and they were together. They had climbed the heights and plunged down from them together, their journey driving the dark bleakness of

Aldo's death from his heart and restoring to him his strength and self belief. Their lovemaking had touched his soul. But he couldn't talk about how he felt. He didn't want Giselle, whom he loved so much, to think of him as emotionally weak and unable to deal with everything Aldo's loss meant.

Instead he must be strong. He must forge a future for them both out of the funeral pyre which would consume the plans they had previously made. He must prove to Giselle that he was strong enough to make that future for them. He must show her that she could trust him to take the burden fate had dropped onto his shoulders and lift it high enough to enable them to live a life as close to the one they had originally planned as possible whilst at the same time carrying the weight of the promise he had given Aldo. Until he had fathomed out for himself how best that could be done—until he could stand before Giselle and show her how it could be done—he wasn't going to discuss the situation with her.

The last thing he wanted was for her to be burdened by anxiety and worry about the change in their circumstances. He might owe it to Aldo to keep his promise to him, but far more important was the duty of love and protection that he owed to Giselle.

Aldo's death had changed their lives completely, Giselle herself would be aware of that, knowing as she did that he was Aldo's closest living relative. She would know and understand that he was duty-bound to step into Aldo's shoes, of course, since they had both always known that he was Aldo's heir. Technically, yes. But neither of them had ever expected that Saul would be called on to fulfil his responsibility towards that duty. Why should they have done, with Aldo younger than Saul, and married to a woman who had made no secret of the fact that she wanted to bear the future Grand Duke? Fate, though, had had other ideas, and now it was his duty to take up the responsibility Aldo's death had thrust upon him. With Giselle at his side, he would build a new life on the foundations his ancestors had set in place—not just for themselves, but for all those his promise to Aldo had brought within his care.

CHAPTER THREE

THE STATE FUNERAL, WITH all its sombreness and so-
lemnity, was over, and Aldo had been laid to rest in
the Royal Mausoleum, Natasha at his side. Naturally
as Aldo's cousin Saul had been called upon to play a
leading role in the proceedings, being with the heads
of other Royal Houses and the representatives of other
governments who had attended the funeral. And Giselle,
as Saul's wife, had also had her part to play—a part
not so very different, really, from her role within Saul's
business as his wife and business partner.

Now those mourners had returned to their own
countries, and two days after the state funeral Giselle
and Saul were finally free to be on their own in Saul's
apartments.

'Have I thanked you yet for all that you've done these
last few days?' Saul asked Giselle warmly as they sat
together in the private courtyard of his apartment, enjoy-
ing the morning sunshine as they ate their breakfast.

'You don't have to thank me. I wanted to help, and in
truth it wasn't really any different from the socialising
we have to do for the business—although I did feel a
bit awkward at times, with so many of the royals who

attended the funeral assuming that you would be stepping into Aldo's shoes. I lost count of the number of
invitations we got to visit their royal courts. Not that I
would want to accept them.'

'Me neither—given free choice,' Saul agreed. 'But
as we both know Aldo's death means that we no longer
have that free choice.'

Immediately Giselle's smile faded. 'What do you
mean?' she demanded.

'You know what I mean. I mean that I *am* going to
have to step into Aldo's shoes, and because of that—'

'What?' Coffee splashed from Giselle's cup onto her
black linen dress as she fought and lost the battle to control her shocked disbelief. 'You can't mean that, Saul,'
she protested. 'You've always said that ruling is the last
thing you'd want. When we got married you—'

Her reaction had caught Saul off guard. It wasn't
what he had expected. He had assumed that she had
realised what must happen. Now, manlike, his reaction
to what his alpha male brain interpreted as an attack on
his honesty and his ability to elicit her total confidence
led him into immediate and sharp self-defence, through
an attack of his own. 'I know what I said, Giselle. But
things have changed. Aldo's death has changed everything—you must know that.'

'I *must* know it?' Saul's totally unexpected and completely unwelcome declaration had filled Giselle with a
panic that was mixed with anger and a sense of betrayal.
'What I know is that I married a man who swore to me
that he would never want to rule this country.'

'I *still* don't want to rule it. This isn't a matter of what

I *want,* Giselle. It's a matter of what I must do.' What had happened to his plans of proudly placing before Giselle a carefully planned strategy for what he hoped for their future and the future of the country? 'You said that Aldo's death meant that the country would need a strong leader,' Saul reminded Giselle.

'Yes, I did,' Giselle was forced to admit. 'But I didn't mean that *you* should take over from Aldo. How could you think I would mean that when you've always said that it was the last thing you'd want to do? I meant that the country needed to elect a democratically chosen strong leadership? How can you sit there and tell me that you are going to step into Aldo's shoes? It goes against everything you've said to me—everything I've believed and trusted about you. I feel that I can't have ever really known you.' The strength of her emotions made her voice tremble and filled her eyes with tears.

Saul felt his heart sink. Deep down inside, wasn't this what a part of him had secretly feared? Even if he had hidden that fear and convinced himself that Giselle *must* know what Aldo's death would mean.

'I can't believe you've chosen to do something like this,' Giselle told him.

'I didn't *choose* to do it,' Saul said quietly. 'Before he died Aldo begged me to give him my promise that I would. For the sake of the country, Giselle.' Saul continued when she simply looked at him in angry rejection. 'He said it was a matter of duty to our people and to our shared ancestry. I realise that this is coming as a shock to you, and that's my fault, but please try to see the positive side of things.'

'What positive side?' Giselle was trembling with rage and dismay. 'You assured me that ruling Arezzio was the last thing you would ever want, and now you're telling me to look on the positive side? The positive side of what, Saul? You lying to me? Deceiving me?'

'I haven't lied to you or deceived you. When I said that, I meant it.'

'But now you've changed your mind? Just like that? Without a word to me?'

'It isn't just like that. I never expected Aldo to die before me, but he has. This country needs us, Giselle. There's so much we can do here—for the people and for the country. They need our help. We can build schools, educate the people, send them to the best universities in the world. We can build a country that values its people, that supports and encourages them.'

The passion and enthusiasm in his voice fell against Giselle's heart like physical blows. 'You've already made up your mind, haven't you?' she accused him. 'You've decided what you're going to do. So much for our marriage being an equal and true partnership. When it comes to the things that matter most you didn't even stop to think about consulting me.'

'I've already told you—I thought you'd guessed. Giselle, I need you to support me in this. I'm sorry if you feel I've failed you. That wasn't my intention.'

Saul desperately wanted her to understand, and to share with him his determination to find something positive in the dramatic change in their future. He hated seeing her so upset, knowing that he was the cause of her distress, but at the same time part of him felt that she could have been more appreciative of his position.

She obviously didn't intend to be, though, because she said bitterly, 'How can I trust you any more when you've made such an important decision about our shared future without saying a word to me?'

How could all his plans have gone so badly wrong?

'I've already explained. I thought you'd guessed… realised… I believed, and I still believe now, that you would see the potential to do good in what fate has handed us, and that you'd want to respond to that challenge, to that demand on everything we have and are together, for the good of others.'

'What about the good we are already doing through our charity, our plans? You can't rule this country and still give the time and the commitment we give to that.'

'The charity has reached a stage where a committee and trustees appointed by us can run it in our place. You know that's true.'

Giselle did, but she didn't want to admit it.

'Can't you see, Giselle? This is a new challenge for us—a new call on all that we know we can give and all that we've already learned about that giving. You are the one who gave me the encouragement and inspiration to begin the children's charity projects. I need that support from you here and now, more than ever. We are soul mates, you and I. We both know that.'

The pain inside her was unbearable—because all of what he had said was true. Just as it was equally true that she could not go with him into the future he was planning. If he went ahead and stepped into Aldo's shoes then he would have to do so without her.

'You talk about *us*,' she told him sadly, 'but it is your intention to take Aldo's place no matter how I feel, or what I say, or what promises you made to me, isn't it?'

Saul ached to take her in his arms and beg her to understand—but he had a meeting to attend, and once she was in his arms their intimacy would not end with a single kiss. It never did. The magical cord that linked them together meant that to touch one another was to want one another, and to prove their need and love for one another in the most intimate way possible. Perhaps it was their mutual lack of physical affection from their parents that meant that the physical intimacy they shared was so very special to them, so cherished by them. Saul didn't know. He only knew that to hold Giselle in his arms was to want to go on holding her.

'I have to, Giselle,' was all he could say to her. 'I didn't want to at first—everything you've said, I felt too. But perhaps there is more to my ancestry than I've ever previously allowed for. Aldo was right; it *is* my duty to do the best I can for the people of this country.'

With every word Saul spoke Giselle's heart sank further and her panic increased—until she felt that her fear was threatening to choke her.

'I can see that I've shocked you,' Saul admitted. 'But please, darling, try to think how much we can do here together, how much we can improve the lot of the people. Please try to understand that this is where my duty lies, where our future together lies.'

'What about your duty to me? To us? You say you promised Aldo you would take his place, but what about your promise to *me* before we got married? What you're going to do changes everything between us. It threatens everything that matters most to me and all that I believed mattered most to you as well.'

'Oh, sweetheart.' Saul was remorseful as he heard the anxiety in her voice, guessing that what was worrying her was the personal freedom she felt they would lose to their shared royal duty. Saul had no intention of allowing that to happen. 'My taking Aldo's place here doesn't affect us or our relationship. I would never allow anything to do that,' he assured her. 'I know that this change in our plans must seem daunting, but we shall still be us, Giselle. Our love for one another won't change. I would never let it.'

Giselle's reaction to his news was not the one he had hoped for, Saul admitted, but he wasn't going to let her antagonism towards it come between them. As a successful businessman he knew that sometimes plans had to be changed at a moment's notice, and that in order to survive in a modern and highly competitive business market a person needed to adapt, to see opportunities and not problems, and to change any problems into opportunities. He had believed that Giselle shared that mindset, but now her refusal to take on board the opportunities for the greater good that lay in this change in their circumstances was creating a barrier between them, and Giselle, with her angry accusations, seemed determined to enforce it. He was a man who was used to taking control and exercising that control—and he was determined to do that now.

'This isn't helping either of us,' he told her firmly. 'I accept that I made an error of judgement in believing that you had already guessed what had happened and were with me in this change to our lives and the way forward. I should have checked that I was right instead of simply assuming I was. I acknowledge that you've every right to be angry with me about that, but accusing me of not considering our relationship—our marriage—and not putting it first is neither fair nor honest. Nothing about what we share has changed or can be changed by outside circumstances. Only you and I have the power to do that.

'Think about it. Giselle,' he pleaded with her, getting up and coming towards her. 'Think about how much good we could do here together, working for the people. Think about how fate brought us together—two people who shared the damage done to them by the deaths of their parents and all that went with that—and ask yourself if fate isn't once again at work here, bringing us both together again to a place and a time where we can do so much for people who have so little. You of all people can surely understand the sense of responsibility I feel towards these people through my blood? I admit that I did not feel or think like this in the past, and that it has taken Aldo's death to make me aware of my duty, but now that I am aware of it I cannot walk away from that duty—' He broke off and shook his head.

'I have to go. I've got an appointment with the senior members of Aldo's government in ten minutes. We'll have to finish talking about this later, but whilst I am gone please try to think positively about the future. You mean everything to me, Giselle. Without you I have and am nothing. Your love sustains me and supports me. You are my life.'

He was gone before she could say anything.

After Saul had gone Giselle paced the courtyard, her heart pounding, her thoughts in chaotic panic. She was oblivious to the sunshine and the tranquil symmetry of the elegantly designed outside living space that had so pleased her less than an hour earlier.

Saul had been at pains to reassure her over and over again that the fact that he was stepping into Aldo's shoes did not and could not in any way alter their relationship, but he was wrong. Very wrong. Because what he had done would destroy it.

What *Saul* had done? Giselle's body shook with the force of her emotions. This was her punishment for deceiving him—for not telling him the full truth about her past and the dark and dangerous secret that lay there. She had gambled with fate and she had lost. Just as she would now lose Saul.

Grief and despair filled her, seizing her body and her mind. Was it selfish of her to wish that Aldo had not died? To wish that she could turn back the clock—to where? To the day of their marriage, when her great-aunt had asked her if she had told Saul everything and she had replied yes? To before then? To her own childhood? Before that? Did she wish that she herself had never been given life?

Yes, when the price of that life was the burden she was forced to bear—the knowledge of the horror of which she herself might be capable and the fear of passing that horror to her own child, which had made her vow that she must never *have* a child.

Saul's insistence that he himself did not want children was because he did not want to inflict on them the childhood he had had, with his parents always absent. He knew how much the cut and thrust of a high-powered business life meant to him, and that it would of necessity take him away from his own children. It had given her the confidence to marry him. Saul had been totally against them having children—then. Now, though, with Saul stepping into Aldo's shoes, that would have to change. He was going to want an heir—a child that she could not give him. She had no proof of that, she knew, but she couldn't help fearing that she was right. He had already proved, although he would deny it, that taking up his role as Aldo's heir meant more to him than she did. So would having an heir.

Their marriage was doomed, and ultimately it would have to end. Ultimately Saul would cast her aside to marry someone else—a woman who could and would provide him with an heir. A woman who could and would give him what she could not.

Ultimately. And ultimately would she be able to stop loving him? Never! Her whole body shook. She loved him so much that she could not envisage stopping loving him—ever. Another intolerable burden for her to have to carry. What was life if all it held was pain and loss? Better not to live at all.

Giselle shivered. Was *this* how her own mother had felt? Fresh panic swamped her. There was no one she could turn to, no one who could help her. Why had this had to happen? The courtyard and the palace itself now felt like an alien unwelcoming environment—a place where she did not want to be because she could never provide what it represented: continuity, a title, a place in life and a duty to be handed down from generation to generation, father to child, be that child a son or a daughter. History was rich with women who had proved to be strong rulers. A daughter! Another sick shudder savaged her. She needed to escape—from her thoughts and from the palace itself, with all that it represented.

The summer sunshine was warm on Giselle's back as she emerged from an ancient cobbled narrow alleyway into one of the city's many squares. This one was surrounded by the historic merchants' halls of the country's medieval trade guilds—the Goldsmiths' Hall, the Tanners' Hall, and others, including the imposing Guild Hall itself. As an independent country, Arezzio, with its rich farmlands and its mountains with their mineral deposits, had traded profitably during the medieval era, the wealth it had earned enabling its rich citizens to become patrons of painters and sculptors, many of whom had travelled to Florence and other parts of Italy to perfect their skills. Now, though, the country had fallen into decline, with no new industry to help it to flourish.

Signs of that decline and also of decay were evident in the buildings surrounding the square, just as signs of the country's poverty were evident in its people. Those with the money to do so sent their children abroad to be educated, and those children then made their lives in other countries, so the country's poverty now also included a poverty of intelligence and aspiration.

Saul had been right when he had said that the work they could do here would be important and worthwhile. But she would not be the woman—the partner, the wife—who would do that work with him. A ruler who needed an heir needed a wife who could and would provide that heir, and whilst Saul had not as yet said anything to her about his need for a child ultimately he would do so. He would have to.

From the square Giselle could see the palace, perched high on its rocky outcrop, guarding the entrance to the fertile valley and farmlands of the country that lay at its back, a symbol of Saul's family's role in guarding the people of this country. Democracy could go hand in hand with that kind of tradition with the right man—a man who was gifted and visionary, a man of great courage and even greater honesty. She would have been proud to stand at the side of such a man, but it could not be.

As she made her way back to the palace Giselle knew that, whilst Saul might love her and not want to end their marriage, ultimately he would have to abandon her or his people. She knew too, after listening to him talk about the difficulties that faced the country, hearing the passion and dedication in his voice, that the promise he had given to Aldo would not allow him to choose her. How could their love weigh anything when set in the scales against the needs of so many? It could not.

On her way back she passed the place where before

their marriage she had seen a young mother crossing the street and been transported back to her own childhood. That incident had led to her revealing part of the torment of her past to Saul. If she had told him everything would he have still loved and married her? She must be grateful for the love she had had, for the joy they had shared, she told herself. She must hold on to her memories and be sustained by them. She had no other choice. And for now she still had Saul and his love. For now. And *now* must be what she clung to, to sustain her, *now* must be the time when she filled her senses and her heart with their love, when she celebrated it with Saul, creating memories for the bleak years that would come.

As she neared the palace she noticed absently the activity in the exclusive and expensive dress shop to which Natasha had once taken her. Its owner was ferrying armfuls of clothes from the shop into a waiting van, leaving the shop rails bare. No doubt without his royal customer the shop owner and his goods were no longer wanted.

Giselle felt vulnerable, and so afraid.

CHAPTER FOUR

SAUL'S MEETING HAD required the employment of a great deal of tact on his part, he acknowledged as he made his way back to his apartments. The old brigade of Aldo's advisers—elderly men in the main, Saul's own father's peers in age and habit—might have welcomed his decision to step into Aldo's shoes, but Saul was under no illusions. They would believe that they could continue to run the country much as they had done under Aldo, with its ruler being little more than a royal figurehead. Aldo had been too gentle natured to stand up to them and place his own stamp on the country. Not that they had done anything wrong. They were respectable, upstanding men, but their beliefs and habits were rooted firmly in the past, and were not conducive to moving the country forward.

They had all looked aghast, and a couple of them had even looked disapproving, when Saul had talked about bringing high-speed internet access to every part of the country, refusing to believe that it was financially possible to do such a thing, never mind that there was any need for it. Their reluctance had merely whetted Saul's appetite. He was used to dealing with objections and problems and overcoming them. He *would* overcome their reluctance. He *would* give the people of the country—*his* people—what they needed and deserved.

Right now, though, his chief concern was Giselle. They always worked so closely together, sharing the same mindset in their beliefs and their plans, that he felt the absence of her support as sharply as he might have felt a cold east wind against bare flesh. Her absence from his plans and his hopes for the country hurt. He wanted her to feel as passionately about what they could achieve as he did himself. He wanted them to be in harmony. He wanted to see her face light up with excitement and enthusiasm when they talked about their plans. And whilst he had been listening to his ministers he had hit upon a plan that he hoped would help her to understand and appreciate how much their skills—*theirs,* not just his—were needed here. It wouldn't be emotional blackmail or even worse manipulation of her feelings on something he knew to be important to her, Saul assured himself. It would be something she herself would see at once as being of concern. Something she would agree needed their intervention. Something that they were uniquely placed to deal with via their existing skills and knowledge.

One of the ministers had mentioned a disaster that had recently hit the country, when some mining being undertaken by one of Natasha's father's companies had resulted in a landslide swamping the small town that lay in the mine's shadow. The landslide had also buried the saw mill which had employed most of the townspeople, leaving hundreds of people injured and their homes destroyed. The townspeople were currently living in dreadful poverty. When Saul had asked the minister what was being done to help them, the minister had told him that there was nothing that could be done. There was no money in the treasury to enable them to do *anything*.

The country had no formal welfare system. Help in such disasters relied on the largesse of the ruler and local help. Aldo had been out of the country when the landslide had occurred, and he had been killed before he could do anything about it.

Saul had made it clear to the ministers that this kind of ad hoc arrangement was not good enough. He had also made it clear that the mining company's licence was to be cancelled, and had been told by the minister that mining activities had already ceased and the mining company representatives had left the country.

Saul had made arrangements for Giselle and himself to visit the area this afternoon, and he was hoping that the plight of its people would help to melt her resistance to them making their lives here.

He found her on the patio, her lunch barely touched.

'I'm just not hungry,' Giselle answered when Saul asked her why she hadn't eaten. It was the truth after all. Her misery was making her physically sick, and she felt so unwell in the aftermath of that nausea that she simply did not want to eat. The very thought of food was making her stomach churn with the threat of fresh nausea.

'You should have something, even if it's only a

sandwich,' Saul told her. 'We've got a busy afternoon ahead of us, with a long drive.'

Giselle shook her head before querying, 'A long drive? Where to?'

'There's something I want you to see,' Saul answered obliquely. 'We've never been in the country long enough on our previous visits for you to see much of what lies behind the palace and the city.'

'According to Natasha it's all countryside populated by peasants,' Giselle told him wryly.

'If the people of Arezzio are peasants then that's because they have never had the opportunity to be anything else.' Saul defended the population. 'I intend to change that. When I was talking to the ministers this morning about the need for countrywide high-speed internet access they looked at me so blankly that I wondered if some of them don't even know what a computer is. I knew they were set in their ways, but I confess that I hadn't realised quite how nineteenth-century, never mind twentieth-century, some of those ways actually are.'

Saul was smiling as he spoke—trying to jolly her along, Giselle guessed, and her heart ached both with love for him and fear at the thought of the future and what it might hold.

Sooner or later Saul was bound to want to discuss the subject of them producing an heir. He would have to do so, surely? Aldo had always made it plain that producing an heir was very important to anyone who ruled Arezzio. When Saul did the same she would have to tell him the truth about the secret she had kept from him.

* * *

Giselle was pleased and relieved when she discovered that they would be on their own in the car which Saul had been provided with, and that he would be driving it.

'They did want to supply us with a driver, but I know the country from the long holidays I spent here in my teens,' Saul told her in response to her comment that she was glad they were able to go out without any undue pomp or formality, adding, 'I've already made it clear to the ministers that I have no intention of hiding myself away behind layers of court procedure and protocol. One of the first things I want to set in motion is the establishment of a democratic voting system, so that ultimately the people can elect their own government, with the right to make its own laws. The royal role will be modernised to that of hereditary Head of State.'

'Democracy *and* high-speed internet access? You aren't taking on much, then.' Giselle couldn't resist teasing him as they got into the four-wheel-drive vehicle parked waiting for them with the keys in it.

The breadth of his vision and his determination to achieve the goals he set for himself were aspects of Saul's character that Giselle really admired. Saul didn't just talk about things needing to be done, he actually got them done. She always felt when she listened to Saul talking about his plans that there was so much she could learn from him—especially about not accepting limitations.

His laughter reminded her of the fun they had always had together, and the way their minds thought alike. It wasn't just her husband and her lover she was going

to lose. It was her best friend and her mentor as well.
And as for not accepting limitations… There were some
limitations that even Saul could not overcome, Giselle
reminded herself bleakly.

Once they were in the car, as though he had picked up
on something of her thoughts, Saul turned to her and told
her, 'It's good to see you smile again. I was beginning
to think I'd lost my best friend and the only person who
truly understands how I feel about things. I never want
to lose that aspect of our relationship, Giselle. In fact I
never want to lose anything from our relationship.'

Nor did she—but they *were* going to lose one another.
They would have to. When he heard what she had to
say, what she had previously concealed from him, Saul
would turn away from her. He would have to now that
he had agreed to rule Arezzio. She wasn't going to think
about that now, though, Giselle told herself fiercely. She
was going to try to concentrate on the here and now,
on being here with Saul, and on him being excited and
enthused about his plans.

She had no idea what he wanted to show her and she
knew better than to ask. Saul had his own way of
working.

Once they were out of the city, and heading south
across the agricultural plain of the wide river that flowed
ultimately into the Adriatic, Giselle couldn't help com-
menting. 'I'm surprised that more isn't made of the
potential of this land to grow crops that could be sold
abroad, given the country's climate.'

'I agree. In fact that was something that I had already
mentioned to Aldo as a potential means of increasing the

country's financial viability—especially with regard to the potential for export—but he felt that the cost of upgrading machinery and educating landowners was more than the exchequer could bear. It is something we should look into, though. The valley enjoys a fairly temperate climate, and with the kind of modern greenhouses the Dutch are using we could easily become a major player in exporting salad and fruit crops, even flowers. With so many new tourist destinations coming into being in Croatia and Montenegro we'd have an easily accessible market there, for a start.'

As he finished speaking Saul reached for Giselle's hand and lifted it to his lips, kissing it tenderly before saying, 'You are everything I could ever want in the woman I love and I am truly blessed to have found you, Giselle. I know that right now you are disappointed in me. You feel that I've let you down, and I feel that too. Those are my errors and my responsibility, but you, my love, I hope will find the kindness and the magnanimity of spirit to overcome the difficulties I have created for us.'

'Because you think I love you too much not to, you mean?' Giselle accused him wryly, adding before he could answer her. 'Well, it is true, Saul. I do.'

'But you are not happy to love me to such an extent?' he asked.

'I am not happy to think you would ride roughshod over my views,' was all Giselle felt able to commit herself to saying.

She simply couldn't bring herself to tell him that between them, via her deceit and the keeping of a hidden secret, and his denial of a promise he had made her because of his duty to Arezzio, they had both set in motion a situation that would rip apart the love that meant so much to them both.

Hers was the greater blame, though. She had known when she married him that she was keeping something from him that in reality she should have told him. And risk losing his love? Have him turn from her in horror? He hadn't wanted a child then. The secret she had kept from him had not mattered. But it mattered now.

They had left the valley's plain behind them now, and were travelling a winding road that circled the steep mountainsides, passing through small villages with stone buildings with exposed timbers, whose inhabitants looked as though they were lost in time. An ancient viaduct straddled two valleys up ahead of them.

'Roman,' Saul told her briefly, following her gaze. 'Aldo and I used to dig around its footings, hoping to find Roman artefacts. There are some in the palace. Maybe we should think about inviting specialists to come and do a dig? Napoleon Bonaparte's armies marched through here, before him the Romans, and before them, so it's said, Alexander the Great.'

'The people look so poor,' was all Giselle could trust herself to say, as she watched an elderly woman walking through a dusty village alongside a heavily laden donkey.

'That's because they are,' Saul replied. 'Aldo was acutely conscious of the poverty of the people, but sadly he focused on attempting to improve his own personal finances, so that he could put more money into the exchequer, rather than focusing on finding ways to help the people to help themselves.'

'And of course those of his financial ventures which were connected to his father-in-law failed disastrously.' Giselle hesitated. 'Wouldn't it be possible to use some of Natasha's father's wealth to help the people?'

'That money is tainted,' Saul reminded her. 'I don't want to build the future of the people on such foundations.'

Giselle nodded her head. It was typical of everything she knew about Saul that he should feel like that. He was a man of strong principles, even if those principles sometimes made his judgement a little rigid. As it would be when he judged her?

The pain that she now had to live with had her heart thudding into a flurry of anxious beats. Think about something else, she told herself. Think about the people and their problems. Think about anything other than the unhappiness that lies ahead.

Although she had now seen the poverty in which this ordinary people of the country lived, nothing had prepared Giselle for what she saw when eventually they rounded the curve of one thickly wooded mountain and dropped down into a small town—the country's largest town after the capital city, Saul told her grimly, after he had stopped the car. They were both able to see the devastation below them, where what looked like an entire hillside had simply collapsed and fallen onto the town, covering over a third of it with earth and rocks.

'What happened?' Giselle asked Saul, appalled.

'A landslide brought on by unchecked and unsafe

mining, allied to heavy rainfall.' He paused and then told her quietly, 'The area's only other source of income came from logging. The landslide buried the logging mill and many of those who worked in it, as well as destroying houses that were in the same area. In all, nearly a third of the population lost their lives. Many of those who survived have lost their homes and close family members. They have lost hope as well. Hope and belief—in themselves and in their country. You and I working together could give them back those things, Giselle, as we have done for other people in other crisis and disaster situations.'

Giselle swallowed hard.

'We can head back now, if you wish,' Saul offered.

Giselle hesitated. She knew that if she saw those people, so much in need, she would not be able to turn her back on them—and she knew that Saul knew it too.

'No. It's too late to turn back now,' Giselle told him.

Giselle was no stranger to disaster areas, or to people in need, but to see so many children, some of them dressed in clothes that were almost rags, all of them looking pinched and hungry as they stared at them in silence, tore at her heart and her conscience. If she had not known that they could do something to help, their presence here would have been an affront, an insult to their plight, Giselle acknowledged. The Mayor of the town, hastily summoned once Saul had introduced himself, kept bowing low to him. His words in the local language might be alien to Giselle, but their meaning and his fear and shame at what had happened to his town and its people were painfully obvious.

Watching Saul speak to him in his own language and then raise him up from his kneeling position increased Giselle's pity for him.

'I have told him that what happened was not his fault, and that we are here to help, not to blame,' Saul translated for Giselle. 'The problem for the town has been that it is too remote for them to be able to bring in the supplies needed to rebuild, even if they could afford them. The mine paid such low wages that the people could barely subsist, even though they had promised to pay those who worked for them very well.'

'We can bring in the materials needed to rebuild.' Giselle told him truthfully. 'We've done it often enough before. We'd need to find a safe place to build first, though. They'll need homes and schools, a hospital— all those things and more. And they should be built somewhere out of sight of the landslip, so that the people won't have to look out and watch whilst the mess is cleared up. They'll know after all that their lost loved ones are under all that rubble.'

Saul listened to the passion in Giselle's voice, his heart lifting. He had known that Giselle—*his* Giselle— wouldn't be able to resist the challenge there was here. After all he had seen so often already how she reacted to the plight of the helpless, especially when those who were helpless and in need were children.

Giselle found it far more easy to behave naturally amongst children than he did himself. He was always too conscious of the angry and resentful child he himself had once been, seeing his mother give the love he had craved to the orphaned children she'd dealt with in her work, to feel totally relaxed.

Selfishly, perhaps, once he had found love with Giselle his decision never to have children had hardened—because he didn't want ever to have to share her love with anyone else. At some stage, but hopefully not for some time yet, they would, Saul suspected, come under pressure from the old guard of the country to produce an heir. When that happened it would be an issue they would deal with together.

He turned to look at Giselle to find that she was watching a small group of children, their voices raised in obvious anxiety. Half a dozen of them had dropped to the ground and were scrambling on the dusty floor of the school hall in which they were now living as well as learning, with shabby sleeping bags rolled up to make space for them to move.

As she watched, a larger child pushed over a small child who had snatched up whatever it was that was causing all the fuss. The small child, a little girl, made a shrill sound of despair as her palm was forced open. Emotion filled Giselle as she saw what the children were fighting over—a small and dirty plastic toy.

Poor things. The little girl was crying silently, tears running down her too-pale face. Without hesitating Giselle went to her, dropping down on one knee in front of her, brushing the untidy tangle of the child's hair back off her face. She had only intended to comfort her. The last thing she had expected was for the little girl to hurl herself into her arms and cling to her, her small hands gripping her as tightly as small claws as she burrowed against her. Giselle was almost afraid to hold her. She felt so thin, her bones so fragile.

A tired-looking older woman approached them, gesticulating and saying something that Giselle couldn't understand.

'Saul?' Giselle called to her husband for help.

He came over immediately, speaking to the woman and then telling Giselle, 'She is apologising to you because of the child. She has lost both her parents, and whilst her brother has been taken in by another family because he will soon be old enough to work, and he is a boy, they did not want her.'

'How old is she?' Giselle asked Saul.

He spoke again to the other woman. 'She is six years old.'

Six years old. The same age she had been when she had lost her mother.

Gently disengaging from the child, she told Saul, 'We have to do something for them—and soon, Saul.'

'I've already ordered some temporary accommodation. It should be flown in to the airport within the week. Then we'll have to get it helicoptered out here. Luckily it's summer, not winter, but I want to make sure they have proper accommodation before the winter sets in. We'll work together on organising everything, Giselle. I'll need you to design new homes, a new school, and that hospital you mentioned. Luckily we've got the expertise and the experience to handle something like this.'

'Yes,' she agreed. 'But this will be the first time we've reconstructed an entire town.'

'It's a challenge,' Saul agreed. 'But I know it's one we can meet—together.'

Giselle nodded her head.

Together. Surely one of the sweetest words in the English language—even if right now it felt bittersweet to her.

CHAPTER FIVE

IT WAS DARK BY THE time they returned to the city and the palace. The light from the electric flambeaux set into the palace walls bathed the ancient stone in a golden glow that warmed it but also cast deep, dark shadows of hidden places and dangers.

Light and dark, truth and deceit, love and the loss of that love.

Giselle almost missed her footing as they climbed the steps to the palace, Saul slightly behind her as he paused to speak with the major-domo. Instantly he was there, his hand on her arm to steady her, and the look he gave her was one of protective caring love.

She had to tell him. It couldn't wait any longer.

In the familiar privacy of their own quarters she stood facing the gently lit courtyard.

The apartments had their own kitchen, into which Saul had disappeared, returning with two cups of coffee which he put down on the coffee table in front of the matt black leather sofa.

'I want to get started on the reconstruction plans as soon as possible,' he told her, coming towards her. He frowned when Giselle stepped back from him. 'What is it?'

'There's something I have to tell you. Something important we need to…to discuss.'

'What?'

Giselle took a deep breath. 'Now that you're stepping into Aldo's shoes you're going to need an heir. It will be expected of you that you hand rulership of the country on to a child of your own blood.'

'Well, yes, I dare say it will be,' Saul agreed carelessly, as though it wasn't something he had given any thought to. Before she could tell him that she could not be the mother of that heir, he continued, 'But not yet. You and I have good sound reasons for not wanting to have a child, and those reasons still stand. Right now the country needs so much done to help its people that the reality is that you and I will not have the kind of time to give that we both agree a child needs. Of course we will be based here and not travelling the world as much as we have done, but our time will still be committed to the work that needs to be done. An heir is still a child, and a child needs its parents' love and attention. We both know that better than most, Giselle.'

With every word Saul spoke the tight band around her heart loosened a little more. She was being granted a reprieve. Fate was allowing her some precious extra time with Saul. Several years of time, according to what Saul was saying to her, and Giselle had no reason to suspect that he was not being honest.

Saul looked at Giselle. She looked tired and anxious, so he immediately went to her, refusing to allow her to step back from him this time as he put his hands on her shoulders. Their bodies were apart, but still close enough for him to smell her scent and remember how it felt to bury his face against her skin and breathe in the scent of her, as if he were taking part of her into himself, renewing the pitcher inside that he needed to keep filled to the brim with closeness to her.

The intensity of their relationship and what they felt for one another had shocked him initially. Whilst it wasn't quite true to say that he had been afraid of his own passionate reaction to Giselle when he had first realised he was falling for her, he could certainly admit that he had initially been floored by it—even shocked by it. Wanting to be so completely close to another person hadn't been the kind of thing he had expected from or for himself. Emotional entanglements of any kind simply hadn't been 'him'. His childhood, and what he had perceived as his mother's rejection of him in favour of the orphaned children she helped in her capacity as aid director for a major charity, had made him wary of allowing anyone close to him, and determined never to allow anyone to breach his emotional defences.

And then there had been Giselle. Every bit as defensive as he was himself, and prickly with pride too. She had initially irritated him, then she had intrigued him, and finally she had fascinated him, compelled him to want to know all there was to know about her. The way they had chosen to live their life might seem odd to others, but it suited them, met their shared need for one another.

It had been Giselle who had helped him find a

way back to his childhood, to deal with the demons
that waited in his memory of it. The first time he had
watched her interacting with some orphans they had
accidentally come across whilst checking out the site of
one of his hotel and spa complexes he had been angry
and jealous of the attention she was giving them, seeing
in her behaviour a reflection of the way his mother had
treated him. But then she had told him that the babies
reminded her of her own baby brother, and when she
had cried in his arms for the loss of that brother, letting
him see the full extent of the pain she carried with her
because of that loss, his need to comfort her had overruled his other feelings.

Through Giselle he had learned to see and believe
that when they helped orphaned children in need they
were also helping the small, lonely ghosts of their own
childhood.

'When we give to them, we give to the children we
once were. When we heal their hurts we heal our own,'
Giselle had told him, and he knew that it was true.
However, her questions about ultimately passing on his
role as ruler to a child of his own blood, combined with
the look on her face earlier in the day when she had held
the orphaned girl, made him ask semi-brusquely, 'Are
you trying to tell me that you've changed your mind and
you *want* a child now?'

'No. I'm not. I don't want that,' Giselle denied immediately. 'All I want is you, Saul.'

'Good,' he told her, his voice rough and uneven with
emotion. 'Ultimately, yes, I suppose we shall have to
think about an heir. But not yet, Giselle. I'm not ready to

share you with anyone else. I saw how you looked at that little girl. When the time comes you will be a devoted mother, and no doubt I shall be ridiculously jealous of my own child, but I don't want us to have that child yet. I don't want anything or anyone to come between us.'

'Neither do I,' Giselle told him, closing her eyes against grateful guilty tears.

She wasn't aware of lifting her face up to his until he kissed her, and then kissed her again, his kiss taking from her the poison of her earlier despair and pain. In his arms she was safe and protected. Nothing could reach her or hurt her there. In Saul's arms was her home, her place of safety. Safety from the outside world, maybe, but there was no safety from the desire they aroused in one another, and nor did she want there to be, Giselle admitted fiercely as Saul pulled her closer, his arousal obvious.

They undressed one another slowly, in between kisses that grew longer and more intimate. Saul's tongue was curling round her own and then stroking against it, that stroke becoming a thrust that moved within the eager sweetness of her mouth like the demand of a drum whose beat accelerated, turning the ache low down within her body into a grinding need.

Now, as Giselle pressed her hips into Saul, gyrating her body against him, rubbing herself against him, seeking the feel of his hard readiness pressing into her as urgently as the eager juices of her desire for him melted into the heat of her aroused flesh, all she wanted was him.

'Wet…' Saul whispered unnecessarily into her mouth,

when his hand stroked up the inside of her thigh and then slid beneath the lacy edge of her briefs. His fingers parted the swollen protectors of her sex, caressing the smooth slickness that lay within them.

Her breasts felt like hard tight cups of flesh, filled with agonised nerve-endings full of sensual longing, all of which ended in the engorged sensitivity of her nipples. Her need was such that she almost wanted to tear the clothes from her own body, so that she could blatantly reveal to him their need for his touch. Inside her head she was already imagining him stroking her willing flesh, tugging erotically on the tightness of her nipples, first with his fingers and then with his mouth. A soft moan of longing bubbled in her throat, and then turned into a sob of agonised delight as Saul slid his fingers along her wetness to circle the hard ache of her clitoris and then slide inside her.

'No!' Giselle denied, but it was too late. Her orgasm had begun gripping her, flooding her with immediate pleasure, its immediacy telling her what Saul already knew. This would be one of those times when his capacity to arouse her and hers to respond to that arousal would take them both from peak to peak of pleasure, until the heights they reached were so rarefied that being there together felt like standing outside of time and reality, belonging to a world that was beyond mere human.

Soul mates Saul often said they were, and at times like this Giselle truly believed that he was right.

In the lull of her orgasm they undressed one another slowly and with great sensual appreciation, each and every familiar place of pleasure was revealed to loving eyes, lips and fingers.

Saul's erection, its flesh smooth and taut with the desire that flooded it, incited Giselle's soft explorative touch, and her heart started to beat faster with anticipatory pleasure as she took control of their lovemaking, knowing that she held Saul in her power. She smoothed her fingers over his hot flesh whilst he lay on his back on their bed, his chest rising and falling with the fierce beat of his heart as he fought for self-control. A small bead of semen escaped that control, causing Giselle to smile knowingly at him and then bend her head to lick it delicately from him before stroking his hardness with her tongue.

Saul groaned and pleaded with her. 'Stop doing that… unless…'

'Unless what?' Giselle teased him.

'Unless you want this,' Saul told her, taking hold of her and pulling her up towards him.

Triumphantly Giselle straddled him. 'You are my prisoner, my sex slave.' She bent towards him to whisper words against his mouth. 'You can't speak or move until I say that you can. You can only watch.'

Kneeling up, she lowered herself slowly onto his erection, initially simply letting the rosy-red head bury itself in her wetness, and then moving her body so that she rubbed that wetness over and over his erection.

She could see the muscles in Saul's throat cording as he struggled not to move or make a sound, but the pulsing eagerness of his arousal got the better of him, and he groaned out loud, causing Giselle to tut and shake her head. 'Now I'll have to punish you,' she told him, before leaning forward and flicking her tongue against the small hard points of his nipples.

Saul's gasp of raw male pleasure made her smile triumphantly at him as she straightened up and then lowered herself more fully onto his erection, taking a little more of it into her, caressing him with her own flesh, teasing him by allowing him the hot, wet intimacy of her body and then denying him, each time taking in a little more of him and keeping him there a little longer, demanding in a softly sensual voice, 'Are you watching, Saul?'

Saul's upper chest was flushed and beads of sweat clung to his throat.

Giselle laughed and leaned forward to lick them away—and that was when Saul made his move, reaching out to take hold of her hips and wrest control of their intimacy from her, thrusting fully into her and then withdrawing, asking her, 'How do you like it when *you* are forbidden to touch?'

It was a game they had played many times before, but Giselle still shuddered with wild wanton desire when Saul held her and moved her, until the depth and speed of his thrusts overwhelmed them both with the urgency of their need, and their voices mingled in mutual sounds of encouragement, abandonment and desire. At last the final intimate melding of pleasure and release came, bonding them together via the intense convulsions that gripped their bodies.

Giselle looked down into Saul's sleeping face, gently tracing the curve of his eyebrows with her fingertip, and then the bold thrust of his nose. He was such an intensely male man, virile and proud and—yes—sometimes demanding, but the essence of him held an echo of the sweetness he must have had as a little boy. Her smile disappeared, her mouth trembling and her eyes clouding with tears as a mental image of the child she would never have—Saul's child, with Saul's features— tormented her.

Her emotions were so intense and close to the surface at that moment that the tears overwhelmed her. One escaped before she could wipe them all away with the back of her hand, to drop onto Saul's face. Immediately he was awake, his early-morning smile for her changing to a concerned frown as he saw her tears.

'What is it?' he demanded. 'Why are you crying?'

'It's nothing,' Giselle fibbed. 'Just too much emotion.'

'Too much emotion for what?' Saul wanted to know.

'I don't know,' Giselle fibbed again. 'Probably the children we saw yesterday.'

'The children or one child?' Saul frowned.

Guilt burned hotly beneath Giselle's skin.

'It's that little girl, isn't it?' Saul demanded curtly, seeing her guilt-stained face and misunderstanding the cause of it because of his own growing fear that Giselle was tiring of it just being the two of them and now wanting children.

Logically Saul might know that his thoughts had their roots in his own childhood, but as an alpha-man who still sometimes felt unnerved by the strength of his feelings for his wife, he was not always very good at understanding the deepest subterranean currents of his own emotions. He felt vulnerable and he reacted by attacking, hoping to vanquish the cause of the threat.

'No,' Giselle denied, torn between relief and guilt. After all, the last thing she wanted was for Saul to tell her that he wanted them to start trying for a baby, even if deep down inside herself every time she held a child she longed for that child to be hers.

As though he hadn't heard her Saul sat up in bed, the early-morning light coming in through the open windows to their private courtyard emphasising the warm gold of his tanned skin and highlighting the male structure of the muscles beneath his flesh. Saul had the body to pose for any designer male underwear advertisement, Giselle thought ruefully.

'This is what all that talk about me needing an heir was about, wasn't it?' he accused her shortly. 'You want to renege on our agreement not to have children and—'

'No,' Giselle denied again, her voice softening with love for him as she assured him. 'That isn't why I brought up the subject of you needing an heir, Saul. If you want the truth, I'm glad that you want things to stay as they are, just the two of us.'

Saul shook his head and then apologised. 'I'm sorry. I suppose the truth is that I'm afraid of losing you. And because of that I don't want to share you with anyone— not even our own child.'

'Because of your mother?' Giselle said gently.

For a minute she thought that Saul wasn't going to

answer her, but then he agreed reluctantly. 'Probably. Although why I should feel like that about you having our child when my mother never cared very much for me, her own child, I don't know.'

'You feel like that because your mother never put you or your needs first—because she let you know that other people's needs were more important to her than yours. No one will ever be more important to me than you, Saul.' She paused, then, unable to stop her own emotions spilling out, she pointed out to him, 'You're the one who decided that your promise to Aldo was more important than the future we agreed on before we got married, not me. It's only because of that that we even need to *talk* about having a child. You chose to adhere to your promise to Aldo, and that means that you will have to have an heir.'

'And you're still angry with me because we're here?' Saul guessed.

'Not really angry now,' Giselle told him truthfully. 'You were right to say that there is a great deal to be done here for the people, but we were so very happy when we were just *us*.' This was as close as she could come to admitting to her own fear.

'We will always be *us*, and we will always be happy together,' Saul told her firmly, before he pulled her into his arms and kissed her.

They were late getting up, and breakfasted lazily, dressed in thick white towelling robes in the courtyard after their shared shower. When Saul announced that he had a lunchtime meeting with Aldo's ministers, Giselle decided that she would start work on plans for the new orphanage, hospital and school.

They'd used a similar pattern for the orphanages: simple sturdy houses in which they tried to keep siblings together, with no more than ten children to each house, no more than two same-sex children to each bedroom, a bedroom for the house's foster parents, a large kitchen-diner, a family room, and a quiet room where the children could read and do their homework. Each orphanage had its own vegetable garden, which the children helped to maintain, and a central square. In the middle of this was the school—the centre of the children's lives—which would provide them with an education and hopefully a future.

In addition to the orphanages, Saul and Giselle's charity also provided teaching and help for foster parents, and offered mentored and monitored six-month tours for gap-year students wanting to do voluntary work.

Here, building housing, an orphanage, hospital and a school would be more difficult because of the enclosed nature of the town, surrounded as it was by mountains, and the fact that there would not be much land to spare.

It was easy to push the future to one side and concentrate on the immediate needs of the orphans, at least for a while. But her guilt refused to be pushed away for very long. After Saul had told her that he intended to take Aldo's place here she had focused initially on how that would impact on *her,* and on how distraught and filled with despair she felt at the thought of losing Saul. Now, though, after listening to Saul this morning, she realised that she had been so caught up in her own misery that she had not fully recognised how her leaving him would impact on Saul himself. He loved her.

But the human heart could love more than once, and Saul had a duty to his country to provide it with an heir, she reasoned. Which meant that he would find someone else to take her place, someone else to love as he had once loved her, someone else to give him the child—children—she must not.

However, she had missed out from these calculations one very important fact, and that was the emotional damage that Saul's mother had done to him—the vulnerability that damage had left within him. When the time came for her to leave, whilst logically he would understand the reasons why she must do so, deep down inside himself he might well end up feeling that she was abandoning him, turning her back on him as his mother had done.

Giselle's guilt intensified. The prospect of the pain she might cause Saul was a hundred times worse to bear than any pain she herself would have to endure. Now she could see the true depth of the damage her deceit would cause, and how her cowardice, her selfishness would hurt Saul, who was innocent of anything other than loving her and trusting her, believing her to have told him the truth about the reasons she did not wish to have a child.

It was too late now to remind herself of her original vow that she would never allow anyone to get close to her—not just because she was afraid of falling in love, but to protect them from falling in love with her when

she knew the limitations there must be on their relationship. She had known that and yet she had ignored
it, because she had not been able to bear loving Saul
and not being with him. Now she would be as guilty of
causing him terrible hurt as his mother had been.

She tried to defend herself from her own inner critical
voice. She had not meant this to happen. She had believed it was safe for both of them to be together. But she
of all people should have known that human life was not
immortal, and that fate demanded payment from those
who chose to ignore its warnings and its embargoes.

CHAPTER SIX

Saul looked across the room of the apartment they had turned into a shared office. Its tall windows looked out on part of the formal gardens of the palace—the Duchess's Garden, so called because it had been designed as a wedding gift for the wife of a late sixteenth-century ruler. Its classical design incorporated a formal rectangular fish pond and an Italianate summer house. Giselle, though, was oblivious to the view beyond the window. She was working at her computer, her blonde hair clipped up on top of her head, small wisps of it escaping to frame the elegant oval delicacy of her face. Her manner was one of total concentration on the computer screen in front of her.

Despite the fact that he had opened unlimited accounts for her at Harvey Nichols in London and Barney's in New York, Giselle still preferred to dress casually in jeans and a simple top when they were alone and when she was working, keeping her designer gowns for official and public functions—unlike his late cousin's wife, Natasha, who had been almost addicted to shopping and had often changed her expensive clothes several times a day. Saul had frequently tried to warn Aldo that his wife's extravagance would only antagonise the population of a country that had so little money.

But it was Giselle who concerned him and occupied his thoughts right now, though, not his late cousin. She had been very quiet these last few days, almost withdrawn, her mood sombre and reflective. Was that because of the enormity of the challenge that faced them in modernising the country? Was he asking too much of her? Expecting too much in wanting her to share his vision for the country's future, wanting her to work with him towards achieving that future?

At night in his arms, in contrast to her manner during the day, her sensuality burned more fiercely and passionately than ever, her hunger for their lovemaking so intense that he felt they were constantly touching new heights. And yet despite that Saul felt there was a distance between them, like a glass wall so fine that you didn't even think it was there until you walked into it. And *he* was the cause of that wall being there, he suspected, because of the promise he had given Aldo. Because of that and perhaps also because of the discussion they had had about him having a heir.

Where Aldo was concerned Giselle might understand logically how Saul had felt obliged to make his vow, but deep down inside he believed that she still thought of his agreement as an act of betrayal of her. And in a sense she was right, Saul was forced to acknowledge. But what alternative had he had? His cousin had been dying. There might be some people who felt that they could ignore a deathbed promise, but he wasn't one of them.

When it came to the matter of an heir, however, he wasn't going to make the same mistake. Their original discussion had made him think very seriously about the whole issue of the country's future. He had come to a decision, and it was only right that he discussed that decision and his reasons for it with Giselle—that he set them before her and asked for her opinion. The truth was, though, that he wasn't entirely sure she would agree with what he wanted to do. And if she didn't…

'How are the plans for the orphanage coming on?' he asked Giselle, sliding his thoughts to one side and telling himself that the best way to heal the breach between them was for him to show Giselle how important she was to him.

'Slowly,' Giselle admitted, pushing a tendril of hair back off her face as she swung round in her chair to face him. 'The lack of available land is a problem—although I think I've solved it by planning to build in blocks of four, four storeys high, so that they take up less room. They'll be tall and narrow, rather than wide and low. That works with the lack of land, but I'm concerned about different floors separating the household when what we want is to bond the children with one another and with their foster parents. Normally we'd have a large kitchen-diner, a sitting room and a quiet room all on the same floor. With this design there'd be a large kitchen-diner on the ground floor, with the sitting room and quiet room above it.'

'What about a circular staircase going up from the kitchen-diner to the sitting room, in addition to the normal stairs?' Saul suggested.

Giselle's frown disappeared. 'Thank you, that's an excellent idea,' she told him truthfully, giving him a rueful look that acknowledged his skill.

'Team work.' Saul smiled. 'Something you and I are very good at when the team is the two of us.' He paused. 'There's something I want to talk over with you—about the future of the country and about our future too. But if now isn't a good time…'

Giselle's heart started to thump heavily against her ribs. She could tell from Saul's expression as well as what he had said that whatever it was he wanted to discuss was important.

'Now is fine,' she answered. It was almost lunchtime after all, and they'd planned to drive out to what Saul had told her was the country's beautiful lake area, taking a picnic lunch with them.

There was a brief knock on the door and a maid appeared with what was usually a mid-morning indulgence of freshly made filter coffee for both of them. Giselle raised an eyebrow in query once she had gone, asking Saul wryly, 'I take it you think I'm going to need this? So that means whatever it is you want to discuss is something very important.'

She was trying to strive for a light note, but when Saul didn't deny her claim her anxiety and tension increased.

She knew that Saul had recognised her apprehension when he was the one to pour the coffee, blending her own with just the amount of hot milk she liked. His actions reminded her that whilst Saul did not always say anything he was an extremely acute observer, picking up the smallest of details. Had he guessed that she was keeping something from him?

He handed her the coffee and then said quietly, 'What I want to discuss with you is the matter of the tradition of royal succession.'

Giselle almost spilled her coffee. Her hand shook violently with dread. 'I thought we had already discussed that, and that you'd made up your mind that it could wait until you'd achieved other things?' Giselle could hear the defensive anger in her own voice, but if Saul could hear it too he wasn't letting her see it. If anything his manner was that which she remembered from when they had first met: cool, determined, and very alpha-male. The manner and attitude of a man who was used to getting what he wanted.

'Yes,' Saul agreed, the businesslike tone of his voice confirming what she was thinking. 'And that was an adequate decision as far as it went. However, it merely puts the whole issue of the future governance of the country on the back burner, rather than dealing with it. I have to accept that when Aldo asked me to step into his shoes as his cousin and only living male relative, in effect the last of our line, it would have been his expectation that I follow in the tradition of our family and produce an heir—preferably a son I would bring up and train to rule after me.'

Now it was time for Giselle to agree, and she forced out a, 'Yes…' which she hoped was neutral enough not to give away what she was really feeling. To hide her apprehension she raised her cup to her lips, and then had to lower it when her stomach heaved with nausea.

That the very smell of the coffee she normally loved should make her feel sick was surely a sign of her fear and dread.

'I need your help, Giselle,' Saul told her. 'I know what I want to do, and what I believe it is one hundred percent right to do, but I can't do it without your support.'

Such uncharacteristic humility from Saul of all men increased her despair. He must indeed be desperate to have an heir if he was prepared to beg for her acquiescence. But then he already knew how she felt, and she had believed that she knew how *he* felt. Anguished tears she could not allow herself to shed smarted at the backs of her eyes. Saul had told her that he would not want an heir for several years and she had believed him, had trusted his declaration. Just as he had believed her and trusted her when she had let him think that he knew why she didn't want children, when in reality he knew nothing of the real truth because she had kept it from him.

Now he was going to tell her that he had changed his mind and he wanted them to start trying for a baby—an heir. She knew it.

Giselle's silence and lack of response was not the reaction Saul had hoped for, but he wasn't going to give up. That wasn't the kind of man he was—especially not where the principles he held dear were concerned.

'Part of the reason I made Aldo that promise was because I felt and still feel guilty about the fact that he married Natasha,' he reminded Giselle, repeating what he had already told her before adding, 'Yes, I know what you are going to say. Aldo loved Natasha. And that is true. He did love her. But she did not love him, and sadly I think in his heart he knew that. If I had not introduced them his life could have been so different. Aldo would, I think, have been open to the kind of traditional semi-arranged marriage his advisers would have recommended. He might even have had a child by now, and he certainly would not have been killed in an assassination aimed at his father-in-law. Because of that...'

'You want a child—an heir. For Aldo,' Giselle guessed. With every word Saul had uttered she had become more and more revolted by what she was hearing, by Saul's assumption that she would allow any child, never mind her own child, to be used as a living pawn, forced into a life they might not want out of a misguided sense of duty to a family tradition which in Giselle's eyes had no place in modern society.

The strength of those feelings overwhelmed her guilt and despair for herself. What Saul wanted to propose ran counter to everything she had believed about him, the democratic beliefs she had thought they shared. Her fury at his betrayal was every bit as strong as though he had betrayed her with another woman, and her voice was filled with angry passion and contempt as she told Saul, 'Even if I wanted to have a child I would never agree to having one because you feel you owe it to Aldo. I would never sacrifice my child on the altar of your deathbed promise to your cousin, trapping him or her into such a set role even before they are conceived, never mind born. I won't agree, Saul. Not because I don't want children, but because I could never agree to...to the sacrifice of any child into a life of such rigidity that they can never be free to make their own choices.'

Tears of angry disappointment at him and his values blurred her vision, turning Saul into a tall dark shape whose expression she could not see. She could guess how he was looking, though. He would be staring at her with the same grim hostility she had seen in his eyes the first time they had met and she had stolen his parking spot. Then she had been the one morally at fault, but this time that position was his. She wanted to cry with grief, but she wasn't going to go back on what she had said. She couldn't.

'I don't want to talk about this any more,' she told Saul. 'In fact I couldn't. I dare say I have made you angry, Saul, but you have disappointed me. I've come to accept that there is something in your blood and in your inheritance that means a part of you is claimed by this country and your role in it, but I will not accept or agree to having any part in creating a child because you feel you owe it to Aldo to do so.'

As she hurried past him, intent on escaping, Saul stepped in front of her, his hands locking round her wrists as she raised her hands to push him off, imprisoning her. And then, to her disbelief, Saul bent his head and kissed her—not gently or carefully, but with raw fierce emotion, leaning back against the closed door, ruthlessly dragging her with him, so that she was forced to lean against his body for support or risk losing her balance.

Angrily she fought the domination of his kiss, trying to close her lips against the thrust of his tongue, trying to deny her body its immediate and willing response to the feel of his against it, trying to force back her tears, her emotions, her love for him, until in the end she felt her only means of defiance was to kiss him back as fiercely and passionately as he was kissing her. Sexual intimacy could, after all, express things other than mutual love and desire; it could express bitterness, and contempt, and rage, a desire to hurt and destroy, a desire to…

'How could you think such a thing of me?' Saul was demanding against her lips, his hands clasping the sides of her face now. 'How could you believe that I would ever force any human being, much less a child, into a life they had not chosen for themselves? I could be angry about that, Giselle, but your passionate defence of the values that are so very important to me makes that impossible. I have no intention of us creating a child to assuage the guilt I feel over Aldo. That wasn't what I was planning to discuss with you at all.'

Giselle could feel herself shaking. She needed the support of his body now, seeking it as a form of haven from the turmoil of her emotions and the effect they were having on her own flesh.

'Then what *were* you going to say?' she asked Saul.

She felt his chest lift and then fall as he breathed in and then exhaled.

'What I wanted—still want—to discuss with you is your opinion on my wish that we turn this country into a proper democracy. When Aldo asked me to promise that I would do everything I could for his country I know that was not what he had in mind, but sometimes loving something or someone means giving them their freedom, respecting their ability to make their own choices, furnishing them with the tools to make those choices. What I want to give the people of this country is not an heir but the right and ability to govern themselves. I want ultimately to be able to abolish the role of hereditary ruler and the title that goes with it, and of course one of the best ways in which we can do that is by *not* having a child.

'This country could be our child, our hostage to fate, Giselle. If we want that. We could protect it and guide it and love it, and eventually watch it grow to maturity and an ability to continue on its journey without us, secure in the knowledge that we have provided it with the tools, the education, the love to make that journey with confidence and skill. If it is my destiny to be here in Aldo's place then I shall also make it my destiny to give this country the very best gift I can give to it. But I need your support for that. I need your commitment to the work that it will entail, and I need your assurance that you will not change your mind about our mutual decision not to have a child.'

Tears filled Giselle's eyes and rolled down her face until they met the barrier of Saul's hands. Very gently he smoothed them away.

'You are wonderful, Saul. Truly noble and…and visionary. Of course I'll support you. You know I will. I can't think of anything I'd want to support more than what you are planning.'

'And your assurance? Do I have that as well? It's important, Giselle, because there is bound to be pressure from the old guard here. If we don't have a child then they won't have a prospective heir on which to hang their arguments for maintaining the status quo.'

'You have my assurance,' Giselle promised him. How she had managed to be so lucky she didn't know, but whatever the cause of her release from the torment she had been suffering she was grateful to it. 'I love your plans for a democracy, but you'll face an awful lot of opposition from Aldo's ministers and courtiers,' she warned Saul.

'I like opposition,' he responded with a glint in his eyes. 'You of all people should know that. Remember how you fought against me?'

'Since I had to fight against you, and against wanting you, it was no wonder I lost. And in losing I won the greatest prize of all,' Giselle said softly.

Later that day, sitting on the rug they had spread out on the sun-warmed sand of a tiny lakeside bay, with Saul lying stretched out, his head pillowed on her lap, Giselle thought that this day—this afternoon, this minute of time—must be the happiest she had ever had. Her guilt had been lifted from her, to float away as easily and lightly as the small white clouds high above them in the blue sky, and the perfection of their surroundings echoed the perfection of their love and her happiness in it.

There was nothing for her to fear any more, nothing that could hurt her now. She need not worry any longer about what she had been too afraid to tell Saul because it no longer mattered. She was safe. Their love was safe, and would remain safe for ever.

CHAPTER SEVEN

TWO MONTHS LATER, AS she sat staring at the calendar on her desk, Giselle wondered bleakly how she could ever have been foolish enough to believe that she would escape so easily.

She desperately wanted—no, needed to believe that she was completely and totally wrong in her suspicions, but the calendar could not lie and neither could her body. The first month she had simply assumed that the frightening and unwanted suspension of the familiar regular rhythm of her periods had been caused by the stress and the turmoil of their lives following the shocking news of Aldo's death. But now she had missed a second period as well.

Initially, when her period had not materialised, she had told herself that it was silly to worry since after all she was losing weight, if anything, not gaining it. Nor had she been sick at all—apart from the time she had felt so desperately nauseous when they had first arrived in the country, and that had been caused by the effects of Aldo's death, a long-haul flight, and her fears about the future.

She had certainly not experienced any other changes

in her body that she might have attributed to pregnancy. But would she have deliberately ignored them had they manifested themselves? No, she insisted to herself, because she had not had them.

She knew that she hadn't missed a single birth pill, and after missing that first period she had dismissed the entire matter from her thoughts. Or at least she had tried to pretend to herself that she had. However, as the due date for the start of her next period had grown closer her stomach had started to churn with anxiety. And now that date had come and gone—over a week ago— and still nothing had happened. There was a cold lump of fear and disbelief lodged in the pit of her stomach. She remembered that bout of nausea, and the fact that sickness could eliminate the effectiveness of the birth control pill. But surely she could not be pregnant? Fate could not be so cruel when it knew that she *must* not be pregnant. Not only because of the secret fear she carried inside her head, but also because Saul had made it clear that they could not have a child.

She had given him her promise that they would not, not knowing then that it was already too late and she had already conceived. *Might* have conceived, she corrected herself. She had no proof that she had other than her fear caused by the fact that she had now missed two periods. She didn't feel pregnant, and she certainly didn't want to be pregnant. But what if she was? She needed to know. She needed to find out the truth—and that could not be done here in Arezzio, where they lived in a closed community in which there still lived a doctor with the title of Royal Court Physician. A bubble of tormented anxiety tried to turn into hysterical panicky laughter in her throat, only for her to ruthlessly suppress it.

She could not carry on like this, not knowing—like a terrified teenager, unable to face the potential consequences of an unwanted pregnancy. These days, though, most modern teenagers were probably far more aware and responsible than she was being, Giselle told herself. She was the one who had been naïve, who had been trying to bury her head in the sand and wanting the whole situation to simply go away. She couldn't do that any longer, though. Not now. She must find out the truth and if necessary act on it.

For that she needed the anonymity of a big city— London—with medical facilities that would enable her to find out the truth discreetly. And just as discreetly to make arrangements to bring an end to any unwanted pregnancy? Giselle shuddered.

Because she had always assumed that she would never be pregnant she had never given much thought to the termination of pregnancy, other than to feel sorry for those women who for one reason or another felt it necessary to go through with it. Such a prospect had always seemed distant from her—the kind of awful decision she would never have to make. But now she might have to. That thought only increased her fear and despair.

She felt so afraid and vulnerable that she wanted desperately to cling to Saul, be protected by his presence. But that wasn't possible. Saul could not protect her from what she might be facing. She needed to go to London.

* * *

She brought up the subject over lunch—a quick salad and sandwich affair, eaten in the courtyard whilst she and Saul went over the progress being made with the orphanage, and other problems still to be dealt with.

'I could do with a few days in London—to collect some more of my clothes and then to go up to Yorkshire to see my great-aunt,' she told Saul as casually as she could. 'There's no need for you to come with me.'

'I need to set up some meetings in London myself. I can deal with most of my work involving the business here, but I do need to see some people it will be easier to meet up with in London,' Saul responded—so easily that her deceit was even more painful to bear. 'So we might as well go together.'

Dry-mouthed, Giselle nodded her head. She dared not insist that she wanted to go on her own. That was bound to have Saul asking her more questions than she could answer—especially when normally she always wanted them to do things together.

They flew into London by private jet two days later, and Giselle had to struggle to conceal her relief when Saul asked, when they sat together in the back of their chauffeur-driven car as it left Heathrow for the city, if Giselle would mind going to their Chelsea house without him. He wanted to be dropped off at the office, so that he could get straight to work there.

'I shouldn't be too long,' Saul told her. 'Shall we eat out tonight? I'll get Moira to book us a table somewhere. Is there anywhere you'd prefer?'

'No, you choose,' Giselle told him. Inwardly, all she could really think about was her need to buy herself a pregnancy testing kit—and the sooner the better. She didn't want to ask the driver to drop her off at the nearest chemist, and she couldn't even risk using a chemist local to their Chelsea home, just in case she was recognised.

Saul's smile and brief kiss as he got out of the car outside the block that housed his company's offices, and his promise not to be any longer than necessary before joining her, only increased her desperation and misery. If only she could just close her eyes and then open them again to find that all this was just a horrible, horrible nightmare, and that in reality she was safe, and she wasn't pregnant at all. She might not be, after all. There was nothing yet to prove that she was.

Nothing except those two missed periods, Giselle reminded herself grimly.

After the chauffeur had dropped her off she went into the house, quickly checking that the concierge service they used had stocked the fridge, and ensuring that everything was ready for them to spend a few nights there—the beds freshly made up with the Egyptian cotton sheets that Saul insisted on, towels in the bathroom, and a supply of their favourite toiletries. Then she hurried out again, taking the tube to Oxford Street with its anonymous crowds, and hesitating apprehensively by the entrance to a large nationwide chemist store before going in.

It was easy enough to find what she was looking for. In fact the choice of pregnancy testing kits was so large that it overwhelmed her at first, confusing her as she picked up one pack and then another, her fingers semi-numb with nerves as she tried to read the instructions. She wanted one that she could use immediately, which would show her equally immediately whether or not she was pregnant. In the end, because she was taking so long and because she felt so self-conscious, she quickly picked up three different kits and put them into her basket, moving further down the shelves to add a tube of toothpaste and some other toiletries to cover the kits as she headed for the tills—just in case she saw anyone she knew. She recognised that she was probably overreacting. That was what guilt did to you. It made you feel hyper-aware of danger and hyper-sensitive to your own fear.

It wasn't the crowds and dusty traffic-fume-filled air of the city that made her break out into a sweat as she stepped back out onto Oxford Street, Giselle knew. It was her own fear and dread. The sudden ring of her mobile made her freeze, and her hands trembled when she saw that it was Saul who was calling her.

'I thought we'd have dinner at that place on Berkeley Street, seeing as it's one of your favourites,' he told her, mentioning an expensive and exclusive London restaurant. 'But it's going to be at least an hour before I can get back home.'

'That's all right,' Giselle managed to answer as she gripped the phone tightly.

'What's all that noise?' Saul asked, obviously able to hear the sound of the traffic and other people on the street.

'Oh, nothing. I've had to come out and get some

orange juice for the morning. The concierge people had forgotten to get some in for us.'

'I'll see you in an hour,' Saul repeated, before ending the call.

An hour. Giselle felt as though her whole body was bathed in apprehensive sweat as she hurried down into the underground.

The rush hour had begun and the train was packed, the heat in the packed carriage making her feel light-headed and faintly sick. Maybe this was it. Maybe her period was going to start. Giselle prayed that it might, fighting back her nausea, wincing inwardly at the sight of a heavily pregnant woman seated in front of her, desperate to look away from her. She was thankful when she was finally able to exit the underground and make her way back up into slightly fresher air.

Despite hurrying, and ending up with a stitch in her side from walking so fast, it still took her nearly half an hour from speaking to Saul to get back to the Chelsea house. Once she got inside she leaned against the closed door, welcoming the cool silence. Her head was throbbing and all she wanted to do was have a shower and then lie down—but she couldn't. She had to do the tests first.

In the master bedroom she read the instructions on the first pack she had removed from the chemist's bag and then went into the bathroom.

Two minutes later, as she waited for the result, she was so nervous and shaking so much that she could hardly focus on the line in front of her as it relentlessly gave her the news she didn't want and had dreaded receiving. She was pregnant.

Frantically she repeated the procedure with both the other two tests, hoping against hope for a different result and falling further into despair when those hopes were dashed. She was still staring at the third telltale line when she heard the front door open, followed by Saul's voice calling up to her.

'I'm home.'

Appalled, Giselle looked at the wrappings she had strewn on the bathroom floor. There was nowhere to hide them, so in the end she gathered them up and simply stuffed them hurriedly into her handbag, along with the results, forcing it closed just in time as Saul walked into the bedroom, shrugging off the jacket of his suit as he did so.

'Why is it that London feels so much more uncomfortable than other cities?' he asked. 'It's actually almost ten degrees cooler here than Arezzio, but it feels more like twenty degrees warmer.'

Giselle forced a smile that made her feel as though her skin was splitting. Even though she had known what to expect, the results of the tests had still shocked her, reinforcing the reality that she was caught in the worst kind of trap.

'I've arranged for us to meet with the head of the Dutch company that was involved in setting up the food-growing greenhouse system in Kent tomorrow. I agree with what you said when we first discussed the whole project—about not starting on it formally until we've got enough of our own people trained to instal, run and manage all aspects of it so that it provides work for the people as well as food—but I do want to have some preliminary discussions with him. I want to find out how much help they would be prepared to give us as experts in this field. And most importantly I want to see if we can get him to take on training people for us.'

Giselle tried to force herself to act normally and concentrate on what Saul was telling her. She nodded her head. The growing project would be a hugely important step towards modernising the country, but right now it was a struggle for her to think about anything other than those telltale tests hidden away in her handbag.

Normally when they had dinner out in the evening it was because they were dining with business associates, and the time spent getting ready was a precious time of shared intimacy during which they discussed the events of their separate days and what they hoped to achieve from the evening ahead. Tonight, though, the normal comfortable familiarity of their shared routine—Saul stepping out of the shower to tell her something, her immediate response to his proximity and nudity making her smile at her own love and desire for him, his teasing comments on seeing her expression, about her being welcome to share his shower—which was the stuff of their married life, the warp and weft of what bonded and held them together, only reinforced her guilt and despair.

She should not be in this dreadful situation. She had, after all, done nothing to deliberately cause it. She had not secretly wished for it or in any way encouraged it.

Being pregnant was the last thing she wanted. The last thing she could be. But she was.

'You smell nice. New scent?' Saul asked, emerging from the bathroom with a towel wrapped round his hips to come up behind her and kiss the nape of her neck, exposed because she had clipped up her hair for her own shower.

His compliment had Giselle freezing. Her scent hadn't changed—it was the same one she always wore—but obviously she smelled different because of the hormonal changes within her body. A feeling familiar from her childhood gripped her. A feeling of sick panic and help-lessness at being in a frightening situation over which she herself had no control. Now, as then, her first long-ing was for someone to turn to, someone to help her, but as before there was no one, and she was once again alone with the horror of her situation.

Perhaps it was no mere coincidence that the first dress she automatically reached for out of the wardrobe which held her evening clothes was black—the colour of mourning—a sliver of a matt jersey in which the pleats and folds, once on the female human body, took on the subtle sensuality that was the designer's hallmark.

Giselle hesitated, her hand on the hanger, but then Saul called out, 'Table's booked for eight, and it's seven now,' causing her to remove the dress from the cupboard and pull it on.

'Nice,' Saul approved, coming into her dressing room just as she was stepping into a pair of high-heeled black sandals.

'It's Donna Karan,' Giselle answered him, her lips

oddly stiff as they formed the words, as though speaking normally was a new task she was having to learn.

'No,' Saul corrected her softly. 'It's you.'

Sensing that he was about to kiss her, Giselle pulled away from him. She did not deserve Saul's praise, she didn't deserve his kisses, and she certainly did not deserve his love.

It was just gone eight o'clock when they walked into the fashionable restaurant on Berkeley Street, with its designer interior. The restaurant operated a no reservations policy, but since they dined there regularly and it was mid-week they had no trouble in getting their favourite table, which afforded them both privacy and an opportunity to view the restaurant and the other diners if they wished.

Having refused Saul's offer of a drink in the bar before they went to their table, Giselle knew that she was going to have trouble managing to eat, but that she must do so or risk arousing Saul's suspicions. *Suspicions*. Even the language she was using in her most private thoughts was the language of deceit and guilt, she acknowledged, and no wonder. She was, after all, being deceitful, and she *was* guilty. Not of getting pregnant. No part of her had wanted that.

She had gone over and over again inside her head how it might have happened, and the only explanation she could come up with was that the sickness she had suffered after Aldo's death must have somehow negated the effect of her contraceptive pills. If she had paid attention to that then she might have avoided what she was going through now. But she hadn't, and now she was going to be forced to pay a terrible price. She and the child she was carrying.

Her heart jumped inside her chest, her agitation causing her to knock a piece of cutlery onto the floor. When a waiter swooped to replace it Giselle tried to still the frantic thumping beat of her heart. Her pregnancy would have to be terminated—secretly, and soon. Not just because Saul did not want a child but because of *her*, because of the shocking and dark secret she held locked away within herself, within her genes. She could not and would not bring into the world a child who would suffer what she had had to suffer—a child who would carry the burden of the darkness that lay within her and which she could do nothing about.

Saul watched as Giselle toyed with her food. She started nervously whenever he spoke to her, and at other times was so deep in her own thoughts that she was barely aware of him having spoken to her at all.

Something was wrong, Saul knew. Her whole manner reminded him of the way she had been when they had first become intimate, when she had still carried with her the fear of abandonment she had suffered as a result of her parents' deaths.

Although the bar stayed open until two a.m. it was only just gone eleven when they left the restaurant and Saul hailed a taxi to take them home.

Saul waited until they were preparing for bed before saying, quietly but firmly, 'Something's wrong. Something's upsetting you. What is it?'

'Nothing,' Giselle denied instantly, and then, knowing

that her denial would not satisfy Saul, added, 'I'm just a bit concerned about my great-aunt.'

'Would you like me to come up to Yorkshire with you when you go to see her?'

'No!' Giselle refused, horrified by the thought. She intended to use some of the time when Saul thought she was with her great-aunt to end her pregnancy. 'I mean, there's no need for you to do that. Not when you've already got so much to do,' she amended, fearful that her frantic *no* might arouse Saul's suspicions. 'I feel guilty about being so far away from her now that we're going to be based permanently at the palace,' she added truthfully, since she *did* worry about the distance between Arezzio and Yorkshire.

'There is nothing to stop us from having your great-aunt come to live with us. We could easily provide her with her own quarters, and help when she needs it. In fact I think it would be a good idea. She has a formidable brain, and I certainly enjoy her company. She plays a far better game of chess than you do,' he teased.

She managed to produce a wan smile in response to his teasing, even though her heart was thumping with fresh anxiety.

'I'll sound her out about moving, although I'm not sure she'll want to. She's made friends with so many of the other residents of the retirement home that she might not want to move.'

Was that really why she didn't want to disturb her great-aunt? Or was she afraid that her great-aunt might let something slip that would reveal her secret to Saul? After all, her great-aunt believed that he already knew the truth, and it would be easy for her to discuss Giselle's childhood and its secrets with Saul without realising that she had not disclosed them to him.

Hating herself for what she was thinking, Giselle walked into her dressing room, where she stepped out of her heels and then removed her dress, before opening the connecting door into the large bathroom that she and Saul shared.

With its double wetroom, two basins and a large round tub the bathroom was a sybarite's heaven. From the bath it was possible to look out of the one-way glass wall into the courtyard garden outside. When it was dark, as it was now, it was illuminated with clever and discreet outdoor lighting that highlighted olive trees and statues, as well as a fountain, and normally there was nothing Giselle enjoyed more than relaxing there. The bath had a shelf that one could sit on, and powerful water jets that could be activated when wanted. She and Saul had enjoyed many a sensual prelude to their lovemaking there, but tonight lovemaking was the last thing she felt she wanted. She didn't deserve the warmth and comfort of Saul's love, and she was terrified that in his arms she might break down and tell him what could not be told.

So instead of a luxurious and sensual soak she opted for a brisk shower, stepping out of it quickly when Saul stepped in, biting her lip when she saw the look of surprise in his eyes as she rejected his movement towards her.

For the first time in her married life Giselle did something she would never have imagined she would want to do—and that was to feign sleep when Saul got into bed, keeping her back to him and her eyes firmly closed. If he touched her now she was afraid that she would break down and throw herself on his mercy.

'Giselle?'

She froze when she felt the warmth of Saul's body against her back and heard his voice in her ear.

'I know you aren't asleep.'

'I want to go to sleep, though,' she told him truthfully. 'It's been a long day and I'm very tired.'

Giselle had never turned her back on him in bed before. They might not make full passionate love every night, but they always touched and kissed and slept close to one another. Inexplicably, she wanted to keep her distance from him. By saying she was very tired Saul knew she meant that she didn't want him to touch her, and something inside him reacted with alpha-male determination at what translated as a rejection of him.

'Perhaps I should try to change your mind?' he suggested, moving closer to her, murmuring the words against the curve of her ear after stroking his hand beneath her hair and lifting it, so that his breath heated the oh, so sensitive and sensual flesh behind her ear.

The temptation to relax back into him and then to turn round into his arms was so intense that it threatened to overwhelm her. Giselle's flesh was so well attuned to his touch, so desirous of it, that it was already responding to the warmth of his breath. Tiny tremors of arousal were already shivering down her nerve-endings. But that pleasure couldn't reach the cold lump of despair pressed against her heart. It couldn't melt the icy terror that lay

in the pit of her stomach. She couldn't give herself to
Saul, take from him the pleasure she knew he would
give her, and not suffer even more guilt. It would be
wrong of her to enjoy anything now, never mind the
intimacy of lovemaking, in the circumstances that now
engulfed her. She didn't deserve to push her deceit to
one side in order to bask in the warmth of Saul's love
and be held in his arms. What she really and truly deserved was the cold and icy wasteland of his contempt
and rejection.

Saul's hand was on her waist. Soon he would be cupping her breast, fondling her nipple, teasing and tormenting her into turning round into his arms so that she
could wrap her own around him and kiss him with all
the passion she felt for him. But that must not happen.

'Not now, Saul. I really am tired,' she forced herself
to say curtly, and she pulled away from him so that she
was lying right on the edge of their large bed, with her
back to him in a pose that was stiff with rejection.

She could feel the mattress move as Saul moved back
to his own side of the bed leaving a wasteland of cold
emptiness between them. Giselle badly wanted to cry,
but she felt that she did not deserve the relief of tears.

It had been almost dawn before she had finally fallen
into a nightmare-ridden sleep, during which she had
heard a small baby crying somewhere out of sight. In
her nightmare she had searched room after room for
the child, only to eventually see her mother wheeling it
away in a pram. She had cried out to her to stop, but her
mother had only turned to look at her, screaming, 'It's

your fault!' before she and the child had disappeared. Now the nightmare had woken her, her body bathed in sweat even whilst she shivered at the same time. She was afraid to go back to sleep after that, but finally she must have done, because when she woke again it was to find that it was gone nine o'clock in the morning and there was no sign of Saul—not even one of the loving little notes he normally left for her when he had to leave before she had woken up.

Giselle had no enthusiasm for getting up and dressed; she would far rather have stayed where she was, with the bedclothes pulled over her head, blotting out the reality of her life. But nature would not allow her to do that. Her head was thumping with a bad headache. She knew there would be some tablets in the bathroom cabinet, but as soon as she thought of taking them an inner voice reminded her that she was pregnant. For the baby's sake she should not take any medication not approved by a doctor.

For the *baby's* sake? There was not going to *be* a baby. There could not, must not be a baby—for its sake as well as her own. She remembered her nightmare, and the painful piercing cry of the child who had disappeared. Her whole body began to shake.

She mustn't think of that. She must be strong. She must not waver. Wasn't there something about unpleasant deeds? If they must be done then they should be done swiftly? She certainly could not afford to waste too much time. She was, she estimated, about fourteen weeks pregnant.

She needed to do what had to be done speedily. She

must find a doctor—not her own private GP, who was also Saul's, but someone else. What did one do in such circumstances? There were clinics, she knew, and telephone helplines. Her headache grew worse, a sickening, thudding pounding in her temples, and for the first time she did feel head-swimmingly nauseous. This nausea, though, was caused by her emotions and not her physical condition, she was sure.

Lethargically she pushed back the bedclothes and made her way into the bathroom, where she showered quickly, barely able to bring herself to touch her body even though her stomach was still flat and her waist still narrow.

Half an hour later she was seated in front of her computer, checking the details of her internet search, which had given her the addresses of several private clinics.

A telephone call to one of them informed her that the first appointment they could offer her to speak with a doctor and the necessary counsellor was not until later in the week. The other clinics said much the same thing, so in the end she went back to the first clinic and made the appointment with them.

Once they had discharged her—afterwards—she would travel up to Yorkshire to see her great-aunt, although her stay there would be shorter than Saul was going to believe it was. She booked herself into a different hotel from the one she normally used—one rather more anonymous. How long would things take? She had no idea.

In the meantime before her appointment there were

things she needed to do. Get some cash, for one—enough cash to pay the clinic bill.

Saul couldn't concentrate on the e-mail he was supposed to be reading. He couldn't concentrate on anything, he admitted, whilst his mind refused to stop focusing on what had happened last night. Giselle had never turned away from him in bed before. Normally she wanted them to be close, to sleep entwined, and she had often commented a little bashfully on how much she enjoyed waking up in the night to find that he had thrown one leg over her in his sleep, as though to keep her there at his side.

'It makes me feel needed and a part of you,' she had told him. But it now seemed, or at least last night it had seemed, that she quite definitely did not want to feel either of those things.

He pushed away his laptop and stood up, his action drawing the attention of Moira, his PA, who came into his office.

'I've just remembered that I left some papers I need at home,' he told her untruthfully. 'I need to go back and get them.'

'But what about your appointment?' Moira asked him.

'Cancel it.' Saul reached for his suit jacket, the movement of the strong muscles of his torso catching the eye of the smartly dressed junior executive walking through the foyer below Saul's glass-fronted mezzanine office and causing her to contrast Saul's exciting maleness with the metrosexual softness of her current boyfriend's less than honed body.

Alpha-men might be arrogant and demanding, entrenched in their maleness with all that that meant, but there was no denying their sexual appeal, she acknowledged, with a small sigh of envy for her boss's wife—the wife to whom everyone knew he was devoted. That was the thing. Once you'd tamed an alpha-male and he had decided on commitment he was yours for life.

Upstairs Saul, oblivious to her existence, closed his laptop and put it into its leather case, reaching for his BlackBerry as he did so. His intention was to tell Giselle that he was on his way home. But then he paused and just looked at the phone, before restoring it to his pocket.

Why? Why was he not phoning Giselle? Surely not because he thought that if he didn't he would catch her out in some way? Saul didn't much like the direction his thoughts were taking and what it said about him—any more than he liked the instinctive hard edged alpha-male egotism that was pushing aside the far less judgemental, questioning and downright suspicious side of his nature that marriage to Giselle had encouraged within him. But Giselle's behaviour last night had been so out of character—like her suggestion that she came to the UK on her own. She had been justifiably angry about his deathbed promise to Aldo—made without consulting her. Did that mean…? What? That she no longer loved him? That she would be unfaithful to him? That she wasn't honest enough to discuss her feelings with him? If there was one thing that Saul could not tolerate it was dishonesty. In anyone.

Giselle was in the bedroom when Saul unlocked the front door and silently glanced into the other empty rooms before making his way there. She was dressed and ready to go out, and would indeed have already left the house prior to Saul's arrival if she hadn't been distracted by the fact that the packaging from the pregnancy testing kits and the kits themselves were still in her handbag. She would have to discard everything discreetly—*secretly,* she corrected herself, with sharp dislike of her own ongoing need for deception. Her fingers closed round one of the positive tests. Unable to stop herself, she took it out of her handbag, driven by her longing for things to be different to look at it again, as though by doing so she could somehow change what it said and undo everything that it meant.

It was whilst she was looking at it that Saul pushed open the bedroom door. Immediately Giselle thrust the tube back into her handbag, her face changing colour as she did so, and her voice unnaturally high and strained as she asked, 'What are you doing back at home? I thought you were going to be in the office all day.'

'Perhaps I wanted to see my wife and find out why she turned away from me in bed last night,' Saul answered without emotion, his gaze tracking her loss of colour and obvious apprehension. She had put something into her handbag when he had walked in. What had it been? Her phone with a telltale message on it? A letter?

'I told you. I was tired,' Giselle responded.

'Too tired to be bothered with me, but not too tired to go out today. Where are you going, by the way?'

'Nowhere.'

Saul's eyebrows rose.

'I was going to the bank, that's all. I wanted to draw out some money. I thought that my great-aunt might need some new clothes and I could take her out and buy them for her whilst I'm up there,' Giselle told him, flustered by his look into saying something that was only partly the truth but that concealed the real reason she was going out.

It was a plausible enough explanation, Saul acknowledged, but for the fact that Giselle hadn't looked at him once whilst she had given it. In fact she was desperately avoiding making eye contact with him.

Beneath the suspicion that had brought him home and the anger that was now burning inside him, Saul could also feel pain. Of all the people he knew, Giselle was the one person he had believed would not lie to him. Not ever.

'Have lunch with me, and then we'll go to the bank together,' he offered, testing her.

'*No.* I mean, I'd love to—but I know how busy you must be.'

That immediate no had been a bad mistake, Giselle knew. She could see that from Saul's reaction. He was now striding towards her, a very grim look indeed on his face. In her panic her handbag slipped from her perspiration-damp hands. The not-quite-closed clasp gave way as it hit the floor, the impact disgorging some of the bag's contents in a tangle of packaging, lipstick, and— Her heart leapt inside her chest on a surge of wild panic as she spied the telltale test lying half-concealed by its packaging.

Frantically she dropped to her knees, but she was too late. Saul had got there first and was gathering everything up. Kneeling on the carpet, facing him, Giselle saw first the confusion and then the realisation dawn in his gaze as he picked up the test kit and looked at it. Then he turned to look at her, to demand almost too quietly, 'Does this mean what I think it means?'

'If you're asking if I'm pregnant, then, yes, I am,' Giselle was forced to confirm. 'Don't look at me like that,' she begged him. 'It wasn't deliberate. Being pregnant is the last thing I want. It's the last thing I've ever wanted.'

'Then how come you *are?*' Saul demanded bluntly, as he fought against the shock he was too angry and proud to allow her to see. Giselle had deceived him. She had become pregnant totally against his wishes whilst pretending to agree with him about them not having any children. He had trusted her and she had deceived him. She had tricked him. That was something Saul's pride could not tolerate.

'I don't know how it happened.' Giselle defended herself. 'I wasn't very well just after we flew back from the island, and sickness can effect the efficiency of the pill. It's the truth,' she insisted, when she saw the way he was looking at her.

'How long have you been pregnant?' Saul asked grimly,

'Just over two months, I think.'

'Two months?' His anger and disbelief was plain. 'Am I supposed to believe that you've known for two months that you could be pregnant but you've waited until now to find out? You lied to me, Giselle. You lied to me about not wanting a child and now you've tried to trick me…'

'No, that is not true. I don't want a child any more than you do. I was on the pill. I had no reason to be suspicious or concerned… I just assumed at first that all the upset of Aldo's death was responsible for the fact that I'd missed a period. There haven't been any other signs, like early-morning sickness. I wish that there had been, then all this would be behind me and… I had no reason to suspect that I could be pregnant,' she repeated. 'And as for tricking you… Tricking you into what? Being a father when you don't want to be? Do you really think I would do that, when I know just as you do how important it is for a child to be loved? Yes, I lied to you about the reason I wanted to come to London, but that was only because I needed to find out if my suspicions were correct.'

There was too much conviction in her voice for her to be lying, Saul recognised, and some of his anger abated as he recognised that his outburst had been the result of shock rather than the fact that he genuinely believed Giselle might have tried to trick him into them having a child. He even felt guilty about his outburst. The truth was that he couldn't bear to think of Giselle feeling that she needed to keep anything from him.

'And now that you know that they were correct, when were you planning to tell me?'

'Never,' Giselle answered him truthfully

'Never?' Now he was shocked—and hurt. 'You would have kept something so important from me, when we've always agreed on the importance of mutual trust?'

'For your sake. I didn't want to burden you.' She hadn't wanted him to suffer the dreadful guilt and grief that were now afflicting her. But, manlike, she suspected that Saul would look on it as his role to protect her, not the other way around. 'I didn't feel it was right to involve you,' she continued, adding miserably, 'There wouldn't have been any point. I know your views. Your reactions now have underlined them. The problem is mine, not yours, since it is contained within *my* body.'

'And you would never have said anything to me?'

Giselle stood up and walked to the window. 'It's my problem,' she repeated. 'I'm the one who is pregnant, so it's up to me to make the arrangements. To…to make things as we agreed they should be.'

Saul discovered that he didn't very much like the image of himself her words were conjuring up in his own conscience.

'Is it? Or were those conversations you instigated about my need for an heir brought about because you already knew that you were carrying my child?'

His pride was making him defend himself from the unpalatable image her words had caused him by attacking her. But his pride could not ease his conscience, nor his concern for Giselle herself.

'No!' White-faced, Giselle turned to confront him.

'No. You keep doing this. You keep accusing me of secretly wanting a child and forcing one on you when that's the last thing I would do.'

The look on Saul's face said that he didn't wholly believe her. Seeing it, Giselle felt her self-control snap. Pain flooded through her, undermining her strength and her intentions. She couldn't bear any more. She told him fiercely, 'You are *so* wrong, Saul. So very, very wrong. And I'll tell you why. Even if I did want a child I can't have one. And that's why I instigated those conversations about your "need for an heir," as you put it. Because if you *had* wanted one then...'

'Then what?' Saul demanded. 'I want the truth, Giselle, all of it.'

She was caught in a trap of her own making, Giselle realised. 'Then you would have had to find someone else to have that child. Because I could not be its mother—for its sake and for yours,' she told him wildly. 'And as for the truth...'

Tears stung her eyes like minute pinpricks of glass. She had fought so hard and for so long to keep her secrets, so that she could protect those she loved—first her mother and her father, and now Saul—but her strength was gone, sucked away by Saul's accusations and the shock of her pregnancy. Still, she tried desperately to cling on to her determination never to let anyone else know what tormented her.

'You know the truth. I am pregnant with a child that you don't want and I can't have. I intend to end that pregnancy so that I can keep the promise I made to you.'

'You're lying to me, Giselle. There is something more

to this. I can sense it, no matter how much you might try to deny it.'

When she looked at Saul she could see hostility and wariness in his eyes, along with disbelief. The pain of seeing those emotions in the eyes of the man she loved, in the eyes that normally looked on her with love, took the last of her strength from her. She was too weak to keep back the truth any more, and part of her longed to be rid of the burden—to be able to stand free of it no matter what the cost. She owed it to Saul to stand away from the protection of hiding her deceit and let him see her—not just as she was, but as what she could become.

'Very well,' she told him tiredly. 'If you want the truth then you shall have it.'

And then she would see him look at her with horror and rejection before he walked away from her for ever.

She took a deep breath and Saul stood up. 'I lied to you by default, Saul, when I let you think you knew there was all there was to know about my mother and my childhood.'

Whatever he had been expecting to hear it wasn't this, Saul acknowledged. They had surely dealt with all the trauma Giselle had suffered through her mother's death and that of her baby brother in a road traffic accident before they had married. 'If you are going to tell me that you still feel to blame because you were safe and unharmed whilst they were killed in the accident...'

He didn't know that what she carried within her would destroy their lives together and their love. He didn't know because she had lied to him. He did not know what she really was: a potential madwoman and a child-killer.

'It wasn't an accident.'

CHAPTER EIGHT

THE FLAT CONVICTION in Giselle's voice made the hairs
rise up on the nape of Saul's neck. There was a haunted,
agonised look on her face, a bleakness and pain that
made him want to go to her, but the minute he stepped
towards her she stepped back, lifting her hand as though
to ward him off.

'Giselle,' he protested. 'I know how badly their deaths
affected you—quite understandably.'

As though she hadn't heard him Giselle continued
in the same flat tone. 'My mother committed suicide.
She took her own life and my baby brother's life and
she would have taken mine as well if she could. She
tried to before…before my brother was born—when I
was only a baby myself. She'd taken some pills and she
was going to smother me, but my father found her and
stopped her.

'It was having us that did it—having children. It sent
her mad. Lots of women suffer from postnatal depression, but my mother's was very bad. A form of psychosis.
She couldn't help it. She thought that by killing us and
herself she would be keeping us safe. She was supposed
to be taking some medicine to make her well. My father

had even got a nurse living in. She was supposed to be there to help my mother with the baby, but really she was there to protect him. You see, the specialist Dad consulted had told him that after Mum tried to commit suicide the first time it wouldn't be wise for her to have another child. According to my great-aunt, though, after she'd recovered from my birth and the mental problems it caused her, she wanted to show my father that she was completely well. She wanted to have another child to prove to him that *I* had been the cause of her problems because I was a difficult child. My father loved her so much that in the end he gave in.

'Apparently throughout her pregnancy she was on top of the world. I was too young to remember. She was so excited about the birth that my father thought everything would be all right. He loved her, you see, and he believed her when she told him that it was me being a difficult child that had caused her depression.

'She didn't want to have Nurse Edwards living with us. She wanted to do everything for Thomas herself. Then one day Nurse Edwards found him lying face-down in his cot, struggling to breathe. My mother said that *I'd* done it, because I was jealous of him. She wanted my father to send me away. I can remember him talking to me about it. Telling me that I must be an especially good girl and not upset my mother. He said that he wanted me to love Thomas and always make sure that he was safe and well.'

Giselle paused to look out of the window, but Saul knew that her thoughts—the whole of her, in fact—was back in the past.

There had been several times during her outburst when he had wanted to stop her, to comment and question, and most of all to reach for her and reassure her, but he had made himself stay silent, concerned that any interruption from him would cause her to stop talking and refuse to continue. So many different emotions had gripped him whilst he listened to her. Initially there had been astonishment, then a shocked awareness of how she must have suffered as a child, followed by anger that she'd had to suffer. He'd felt guilt too, because he hadn't realised that there might be more to her mother's death than she had told him.

'The day it happened my father was called out unexpectedly to an emergency,' Giselle continued quietly. 'It was Nurse Edwards' day off. Before he left the house my father told me he wanted me to promise him that I would look after my mother and Thomas. I said that I would.' She stopped speaking again, before turning to Saul and telling him emotionally, 'I gave him my promise but I failed to keep it. When my mother said that we had to go out I didn't want to go, but she insisted. I should have stopped her—'

'No, Giselle—' Saul broke in, forced to when he saw how upset she was, stepping forward and continuing to step forward when she backed away from him, until she couldn't move any further because of the wall behind her. 'No.' He put his hands on her arms, his heart aching for her when he felt the rigid tension of her body.

'Yes.' She overruled him. 'Yes, I should have stopped her.'

'You were six years old,' Saul reminded her, repeating

what he had said to her when she had first revealed to him her guilt over her mother's and brother's deaths.

'I promised my father and I broke that promise. I gave *you* a promise too, Saul, and I promise you that I won't break that promise. I should have told you about my mother before we got married. My great-aunt believes that I did, but I was so afraid that you wouldn't want me any more if you knew. What man wants to marry a woman with madness in her genes?'

'Postnatal depression isn't madness,' Saul corrected her. 'From what I've read it happens to many women, and it can be treated, cured.'

'Not always. Not when it's as serious as it was with my mother—and, according to my great-aunt, *her* mother before her, although she did not suffer from it quite as badly. But then it wasn't recognised so readily in those days. My father was warned that my mother's case was serious, because of her behaviour after my birth.

'All my life I've told myself that I can never fall in love or risk having someone fall in love with me, because it wouldn't be fair to them. I knew that I could not risk having a child I might try to kill, as my mother tried to kill me—and succeeded in killing my brother. And then I met you, and I fell in love with you so fast that it was too late for me to do anything to stop it. But not too late to stop you from being affected by the… the faulty destructive genes I've inherited. You said that you didn't want children and would never want them, and I thought that fate was sparing me because I'd been punished enough. I was so happy, even though I knew that I wasn't being honest with you.'

'You should have told me.'

'Yes, I should,' Giselle agreed. 'Because if I had you would have been spared this. You would never have married me.'

'That wasn't what I meant. You should have told me because I love you, Giselle, and it hurts me to think that you've suffered all this without me knowing. It hurts my pride as a man to know that you have shouldered such a burden. As the man who loves you, I should have been shouldering it with you. It hurts me too that you felt you couldn't trust me or my love enough to be honest with me and let me share your burden.'

As Saul spoke tears began to fill Giselle's eyes and slip down her face. Very tenderly Saul wiped them away, drawing her carefully into his arms.

'You must have been so hurt and so afraid.' He could hardly bear to think of the torment she must have suffered as a child, not understanding her mother's behaviour, but feeling guilty after her death because she hadn't saved her, and then later as she grew up and began to understand the realities and complexities of the causes of what had happened. He ached to be able to do something to help her. 'I can't think of anyone more sane than you are, my love. Just because your mother—'

Giselle stopped him. 'I dare say she was sane too before she had me. She must have been, because my father would have known it if she wasn't.' She looked at him, and then told him wearily, 'Now you know why the last thing I would ever do would be to try and conceive by accident. I was so afraid when I realised that I might be pregnant.' She had started to tremble in his arms. 'I wanted it not to be true so badly. You don't know how it makes me feel to know that if I had a child I might end up wanting to kill it. My mother wanted to kill us because she felt it was the only way she could protect us from the pain of being alive. Like I've already told you, it's a form of madness. A form of madness that can be passed on from mother to daughter and granddaughter.'

Her voice softened with emotion and love. 'I'll be honest with you, Saul, had things been different I would have loved to have children. Especially your children. I would have loved to nurture them and watch them growing up to be everything that I already see in you. But that can never be. I couldn't bear knowing that I might pass it on—that another generation, my own child, would have to carry the burden I've had to carry. The fact that you do not want children has been quite literally my salvation. Just as your love has been the very best thing in my life.'

Saul could only hold her. He felt he could barely begin to understand what she had already gone through even before this accidental pregnancy. Her courage and her selflessness humbled him. He could tell from the longing in her voice that to give up something so deeply wanted in order to protect others must surely be the greatest moral bravery of all.

'You should have told me all of this before. It should have been something we dealt with together.'

'It isn't your problem or your responsibility.'

'Of course it is. You are the woman I love. Do you really think I would want you to go through this on your own? What kind of man do you think I am, Giselle? I thought you knew me.'

'I do know you. I know that you don't want children and that I must not have them. I know where my duty and my responsibility lie, Saul. I've got an appointment in a few days' time at a clinic here in London. It was the first one I rang and I decided to go to them.'

Saul held her even more tightly. Her grief and despair touched his own emotions so forcibly that it was as though he felt her pain with her. 'It needn't be like this,' he told her. 'Yes, I know what I said, and what we agreed, but that was before… I can't pretend that I wanted you to become pregnant, but now you are. Why don't we seek proper expert medical advice about your mother's postnatal depression?'

'There's no point. I know what she did. I know what I might do myself. Don't you see that, Saul?' Giselle could feel her panic growing, and with it her fear. She felt as though she was incapable of thinking logically already, and their child hadn't even been born yet. *Their child*. Pain wrenched at her heart.

'All right, we won't talk about it right now,' Saul soothed her.

'Where are you going?' Giselle demanded frantically, when he released her and moved away from her.

'I want to ring Moira to tell her that I won't be in for the rest of the day. I'll make us both a cup of coffee, and then if you want to we can talk some more.'

'There's nothing else to say,' Giselle told him. 'You

know it all now.' She closed her eyes and said despair-
ingly, 'I just wish so much that this hadn't happened.'

No more than he wished the same, Saul acknowledged. Not for his own sake now, but for hers.

In the end Saul decided that it would do Giselle good
to get out of the house, so he drove her to Richmond
Park, relieved to see a faint smile touch her lips when
she recognised when they were heading. She'd always
loved the park, and they'd often come here to walk and
talk together when they were in London.

At first Saul thought that he had done the right thing.
He had forgotten, though, that the schools had closed
for the half-term holiday, and watching Giselle wince
at the sound of children's voices made him wish that he
had chosen somewhere else, child-free.

When he looked at Giselle her eyes were filled with
tears.

Children. She ached so badly to be able to hold her
own child. She felt so torn, so afraid. It was all very well
for Saul to talk of consulting experts. They couldn't tell
her anything she didn't already know. She had seen what
severe postnatal depression could do. She had experienced its horror at first hand.

Saul pulled her in to his side, his arm round her waist.
He loved her so much, and he felt guilty for not having
sensed that she was withholding something from him
that was hurting her so badly.

The panic inside Giselle was like a physical pain.
And when, engrossed in her own thoughts, she slipped
and lost her footing, her first instinct as Saul grabbed

her and held her steady before she fell was to place her hand protectively against her body, in defence of the life she was carrying within her. Fresh tears filled her eyes and spilled down onto her cheeks.

Giselle wasn't really hungry, but Saul insisted on driving down into Richmond so that they could eat at a small restaurant overlooking the river. He was going to cancel all his appointments and stay with Giselle until it was time to return to Arezzio, he told himself as he watched her toying with her food, her face white with despair and grief. He was desperately afraid for her, having seen the state she was in, but he dared not say so in case it made her feel worse.

More than anything else he believed that they needed to get some expert medical opinions from those best qualified to help them.

It was gone ten o'clock when they got back, and Saul told Giselle, 'You look tired. Why don't you turn in? I won't disturb you if you want to get off to sleep. I've got some work I can do.'

He was saying that to her because of last night, Giselle knew. But right now she had never needed him more.

'No,' she told him. 'I want you to come with me. I want you, Saul. I need you.'

There was a pleading note in her voice that tore at his heart. Giselle, his Giselle, had no need to beg him to love her or to hold her.

They showered together, and Saul's touch on Giselle's body was both careful and watchful. When Giselle saw him glance down at her still flat stomach she shook her head. 'There's nothing to see. If anything, I've actually lost weight.'

Because she'd been worrying, Saul recognised. But she was wrong. There *was* something to see. Her breasts felt different to his touch, filling his hands when he cupped them. Saul closed his eyes against the savagely sharp sense of grief that surged through him out of nowhere.

When he kissed her she clung to him almost in desperation, burying her face against his shoulder, her warm wet flesh slick against his own.

'If you'd rather not—' he began. His concern was for her, not for his own arousal or his own need, but immediately she shook her head almost violently and clung tightly to him.

'I do want to, Saul. I need to. I need *you*.'

It was true, Giselle knew. She needed to drive out the demons inside her by taking back to herself the intimacy and closeness that she had thought lost. She needed to re-establish their relationship, to barricade herself away from the pain she knew was waiting for her. She needed the release that their lovemaking would bring from all the dark bonds that imprisoned her. She needed Saul and his love—more, she felt, than she had ever needed them before.

He was careful and gentle with her, his love for her shining though the restraint he was placing on his passion. But his care for her was not what Giselle wanted. She didn't want to be treated as someone who was vulnerable and fragile. She didn't want to be humoured or cosseted or indulged. That was the way her father had treated her mother, as weak and in need of careful treatment, the lesser partner in their marriage. And she was *not* her mother. Not yet…

She wanted Saul to treat her as he had always done, as a woman whose sensuality and desire for him matched his for her. She wanted them to be two perfect halves of a complete whole, so perfectly matched that it was impossible to tell where one of them ended and the other began.

Saul's tender kiss, as gentle as his careful hold on her body, had her pressing herself fiercely against him, lifting her hands to hold his head so that she could show him how she *wanted* him to kiss her. Her tongue stroked over his lips and then prised them apart, darting quickly and hotly into the sensual intimacy of his mouth, flicking against his tongue, curling round it, stroking it with short, quick movements and then longer, slower ones, until she could feel his heartbeat accelerating to match the frantic thud of her own.

She reached for his hand, placing it against her naked breast, whispering against his mouth, 'Touch me, Saul. Want me, and show me how strong that wanting is.' When he hesitated, she told him urgently, 'It isn't your pity that I need. It's your passion. I need its fire to burn away everything but this—us, *now*. So close together that nothing and no one can come between us.'

Her voice was ragged with emotion, her eyes liquid with it, and the way she was revealing her need to him stripped Saul's own defences down to the bone, leaving

him feeling as raw as though someone had ripped off a
layer of his skin. He felt her pain for her.

When Saul lifted the hand that wasn't cupping her
breast, his fingers wide and spread, his palm facing her,
Giselle placed her own hand against it, finger to finger,
palm to palm, her eyes closing on the surge of love that
swept through her. Saul moved his hand slightly so that
her fingers slid between his, and both of them closed
their fingers into a shared closed fist.

'I love you more than life itself,' he told her thickly,
and meant it.

'You are my life, my whole, my all,' Giselle whispered jaggedly back to him.

This time when she leaned towards him he was the
one to kiss her, until control of the kiss was wrested
from them both by the passion twisting, roiling and
burning inside them. They were a single bonded unit of
intense arousal and desire, their shared need one single
fierce force that linked their bodies together, dissolving
flesh, muscle and bone.

When Giselle touched and caressed Saul's body she
felt the response of his flesh as though it was her own.
When Saul took the tight pucker of Giselle's nipple into
his mouth and suckled on it he felt the waves of close
to unbearable pleasure that racked and galvanised her
body into shudders pulsing through his own.

There was no need for him to ask Giselle when she
was ready. His own body told him—just as his senses
told him as clearly as though she had spoken the words
to him that her need couldn't wait. Lifting her now, he
pillowed her against the shower wall and she wrapped

her legs tightly round him, exactly the way she wanted it to be.

His thrust into her, slowly, drawing out the pleasure, half withdrawing from her before sliding himself deeper against the slick, wet, firmly muscled warmth that gripped and caressed him was, Saul knew, her desire and her need every bit as much as it was his own.

Giselle came first, and Saul's harsh wrenched cry of almost agonised release mingled with her low keening moan of satisfaction within seconds.

Later, with Giselle sleeping in his arms, Saul looked down at her and tightened his hold on her. What she had told him today had only deepened his love for her, made his wish that he could have protected her from all that she had suffered all the stronger. When the darkness of now was over their relationship would emerge even stronger. He intended to make sure of that.

In her sleep Giselle heard the sound of a child crying—the sharp, helpless, heart-piercing cry of a newborn in need. In her dream she could see the baby, so small and defenceless. She reached for it, to take it in her arms, but it wasn't there any more even though she could still hear its cry. She woke up in the dark, her face wet with tears, her body aching with longing and pain. Her baby. She wanted it so much. She wanted to hold it and protect it. She wanted to give it her love, and most of all she wanted to give it life.

CHAPTER NINE

SAUL LOOKED AT HIS WATCH. An hour to go before his meeting with Hans de Kyper. Following his discovery that Giselle was pregnant, and his new awareness of her vulnerability, he had cancelled all his appointments apart from the one with the Dutch businessman responsible for the hugely successful growing programme he and Giselle wanted to replicate in Arezzio. It had been impossible for another appointment to be made.

He had tried to persuade Giselle to attend the meeting with him, reminding her of how enthusiastic she had been about the project, but she had simply shaken her head. Saul was desperately worried about her. She seemed to be growing thinner by the day, her weight decreasing as the misery and despair he could see in her eyes grew.

Soon she would be going to the clinic, and even though she had said that she would go alone Saul fully intended to go with her. He doodled automatically on his notepad whilst he thought about the previous night, when he had woken up to find Giselle crying in her sleep. When he had woken her she had seemed confused, telling him that she had heard a baby crying.

Saul closed his eyes and then opened them again. Giselle had made it clear that had she not had the fear that she might inherit her mother's vulnerability to severe postnatal depression she would have wanted to have children, a child...*his* child. Saul glanced absently at the doodle he had drawn and then tensed. On the notepad he liked to use when he was working at his desk was an unmistakable sketch of a stork carrying a baby.

Saul stared at the doodle for several seconds whilst his mind went into overdrive. Then abruptly he pushed back his chair and got up, calling out to his PA as he opened the connecting door to her office. 'I've got to go out.'

'But what about Mr de Kyper?' Moira protested.

'I'll be back in time to see him. If I'm not keep him talking. I need to see him.'

Before she could say anything more he was opening the outer door to his office, pulling on his suit jacket as he did so.

Once outside on the street he reached for his mobile phone. He had come outside because he didn't want anyone else—not even Moira, who was the soul of discretion—to hear what he knew he had to say.

When he had got the number he wanted and made his call he asked to be put through to whoever was in charge of the clinic.

The doctor to whom he eventually spoke introduced herself as Dr Smithers. She seemed to think that Saul was trying to prevent Giselle from having a termination against her will, and insisted that the appointment could only be cancelled by Giselle herself.

'My wife is merely coming to see you for pre-termination counselling,' Saul pointed out. 'I feel she needs to speak to other medical experts first.'

'Then I suggest it is your wife you should be speaking to right now and not me,' Dr Smithers told him crisply.

Saul sighed as he ended the call. He had tried to coax Giselle into agreeing that they should at least seek proper medical advice on the subject of postnatal depression, but every time he raised the subject she became so emotional and filled with panic that he had felt obliged to drop the matter. Giselle was totally convinced that she would behave as her mother had done, but Saul could not imagine her doing any such thing. Now, having spoken to the clinic's director, he was even more determined to accompany Giselle on her appointment—even though she kept insisting that she did not want him to do so.

Saul headed back to his office. He might not have had any desire for them to have a child—he would certainly have argued firmly against them doing so if Giselle had approached him with a view that they should rethink their original agreement—but the situation they were now in had taken them many steps beyond that scenario. Giselle was already pregnant—by accident, by an act of fate. And an act of fate was what had brought them together. Could he in all good consciousness reject one act of fate whilst accepting the other as a gift he hadn't been able to refuse?

Giselle was concerned about the effect having a child

might have on her mentally. After listening to her crying in her sleep, and remembering everything that she had said to him, Saul was now equally concerned about the effect that having to terminate her pregnancy was already having on her.

He looked at his watch. He'd now got less than an hour before his meeting.

As soon as he got back to his office Saul switched on his laptop. Half an hour later he had the name of a London-based professor who was one of the world's foremost experts in the field of postnatal depression.

Giselle was in turmoil—torment, in fact. He knew that without her having to say so. Her grief and despair spoke far more clearly to him of her real feelings than any words could have done. And, since he loved her so much that he could not bear to see her in pain, he was going to make sure that no stone was left unturned in his efforts to help her.

The professor was currently in America, giving a lecture tour, but would be back in London within twenty-four hours. If necessary Saul was prepared to hire a private jet and fly Giselle to America so that she could speak to him. That was how much he loved her. There was nothing he would not do for her. *Nothing.* And that included becoming a father.

Becoming a father. As the shocking realisation hit, Saul knew that deep within himself, even though he had sworn to Giselle that he never wanted children, there was something—an urge, a powerful need—that wanted to protect the vulnerable new life Giselle was carrying.

CHAPTER TEN

HANS DE KYPER WAS A skilled businessman, and on any other occasion Saul would have enjoyed crossing swords with him as they discussed the terms on which they might possibly do business, negotiating into the early hours of the morning if necessary. But not today. Today, when their meeting stretched from one to nearly three hours, Saul knew he had to bring it to an end. But before he could say anything the Dutchman himself was suggesting that they continue their discussions in two days' time.

'But why do you want me to see this professor? My decision has already been made.'

'Has it?' Saul challenged Giselle softly. 'Have you really made the decision you want to make, Giselle? Or have you made the one you feel you have to make?'

'I know what he will say, Saul. I know he will tell me that I've made the right decision.'

Saul shook his head. 'No, you don't know that, Giselle. You can't know it without speaking with him. You simply believe it. I want us to go and see him, hear what he has to say.'

Saul hated to put pressure on Giselle when she was already so distraught. Tears were pouring over the now too-sharp prominence of her cheekbones as she paced the floor of their sitting room. She was gaunt and thin, her eyes huge and luminous with tears and emotion as she shook her head in denial of his suggestion that they consult the professor. But Saul wasn't going to give up.

'Listen to me,' he begged her. 'You were six years old when your mother died. That's nearly twenty years ago—just think of the leaps and bounds there have been in medical science since then.'

'Science, yes. But this is more complex than that. There isn't a formula that can be applied to put things right. It's a mental problem—a...a form of madness.'

'Giselle, please—do it for me. See him for me—if you won't see him for yourself.'

Saul watched as her eyes widened and then became shadowed.

'You'd do that to me?' she demanded in disbelief. 'You'd use that kind of emotional pressure against me?'

'It's for your own sake—to help you.'

'Help me? And what happens if this professor says that he thinks I *will* be like my mother? Do you really think that knowing that will help me?'

'I don't think he will say that. Because I don't think you will be like her.'

'You can't know that, Saul. Perhaps you're even hoping that he *will* say that I'll be like her. You don't want children, after all.'

'How can you say that? Trust me, please, Giselle. I love you, and I'm trying to help you. Just talk to him. That's all I'm asking you to do. Make an appointment to see him and hear what he has to say.'

'Very well,' Giselle agreed reluctantly. Maybe it *was* only fair to hear what this professor had to say.

The words seemed to hang between them. Giselle's heart was pounding, her emotions whirling, as she recognised exactly what those words really meant. With every day that passed—every hour, every minute—the baby she was carrying was more precious to her. She had thought about things until her head ached from thinking, until she was so confused that she was unable to think any more. It had been simple before she had known she was pregnant to tell herself there could never be a child—for its own sake. Now that a child was a growing reality inside her all the logic in the world could not compete with the fierce determination and strength of her maternal instincts. She wanted this baby. She wanted it with a yearning, aching intensity that was far too strong for her to fight or resist.

'Do you want me to make the appointment?' Saul offered.

Giselle shook her head.

'No. No, I'll do it myself.'

'Here are the details,' Saul told her, handing over the information he had printed out from his computer search. 'Why don't you make the appointment now, whilst I go and do some work?'

Giselle nodded her head.

As soon as she was on her own Giselle looked at

the papers Saul had given her. She felt sick at the very thought of seeing this professor she knew nothing about. What if he confirmed that there was still not a lot they could do? That this rare form of psychosis could still happen to her? She didn't know what to do. She felt sick with fear and panic. But she had promised Saul. She reached for her mobile and started to dial the number on the printout and then stopped. It was no good. She could not do it. She couldn't bear to hear in cold stark words what she already feared. Crumpling up the paper, she threw it in the wastepaper bin.

'Have you made the appointment with the professor yet?' Saul asked a couple of hours later. They were in the kitchen, where Saul was making them both a hot drink—tea for Giselle, now that she could no longer tolerate the strong coffee she adored.

'No, not yet—it's getting a bit late now. I'll do it tomorrow,' Giselle told him. The truth was that she hadn't even tried to make an appointment, because she felt so afraid of what it might reveal.

Over twenty-four hours later, with the appointment still not made and Giselle refusing to give him a straight answer every time he asked her why she hadn't made it, Saul was beginning to worry even more about her. All he wanted to do was help her, but she seemed determined not to accept that help. It was almost as though she had already convinced herself that nothing and no one could help, but Saul refused to believe that. In his own mind he was sure that she would be a wonderful mother.

How could she not be when she was such a wonderful person? He firmly believed that the professor would be able to reassure her and calm her fears. But how could that happen if she refused to see him?

It was past midnight, and Giselle was in bed and asleep. Saul had gone to look at her ten minutes ago, and in the moonlight coming into the room he had seen the traces of tears on her skin.

He loved her so much.

And the child she was carrying? *His* child?

A sensation he had not expected and was not prepared for tightened its fingers on his heart.

They *had* to see the professor—so that they could seek his professional opinion and then be guided by the advice he gave them. The situation was far too important for them to try to make any decision on their own and without proper advice.

Somehow he had to find a way of persuading Giselle to agree to see him. For both their sakes. No, Saul corrected himself mentally, for *all* their sakes. There was nothing else for it. He was going to go ahead and make an appointment for them to see him. He would find a way to convince Giselle that it was the right thing to do.

It was time for him to take matters into his own hands, Saul decided.

By morning Saul had made his decision and acted upon it. He re-read the e-mail he had just received from the professor's PA, confirming the urgent appointment he had requested. The only day she had been able to fit them in was the same day as Giselle's appointment at the clinic, two hours before her appointment there. Printing off the e-mail, Saul left his study to go upstairs, where Giselle was still sleeping. He was loath to wake her, feeling that she needed her rest, but he did want her to know about the appointment. He hesitated, torn between letting her sleep on knowing how exhausted she had been the previous evening, and waking her up so that he could tell her about the appointment in person. He decided that it was best to let her sleep. Quickly he wrote her a note, explaining what he had done, and pinned the printed-off e-mail to it.

When Giselle woke up the first thing she saw was the note Saul left on his own pillow.

My darling Giselle,

You'll see from the attached e-mail that I've gone ahead and made an appointment for us to see the professor. I really do feel that this is the right thing for us to do, and something we *must* do. I know the thought of seeing him makes you afraid, and I understand why, but seeing him will be for the best. I think in your heart you know that.

No matter what he says, nothing can change my love for you. You will always have that.

I love you, my darling—Saul.

The note ended with three kisses.

Saul had gone ahead and made the appointment. Because he didn't trust her to do it? He was justified in thinking that after she had said she would do so and then hadn't, Giselle knew, but his actions still hurt her.

By the time she had read the note three more times she was starting to panic.

She knew every word of Saul's note off by heart now, and her heart was thudding frantically in response to them. Saul was going to force her to see the professor. Saul had told her that he did not believe she could ever be like her mother, but what if the professor disagreed? What if he told them both that after she had given birth she would be a risk, a threat to her baby? What then? Was Saul's insistence on them seeing the professor because really he hoped that the professor would say there was too much of a risk for her to be a mother? She wasn't sure what Saul felt about the pregnancy…she'd been too afraid to ask.

Her head was pounding with anxiety and with the adrenalin rush produced by her body to protect her— the instinctive fight or flight mechanism. Fight? Wasn't flight a better option for her? Flight to somewhere, someone, with whom she would be safe—just as she had been safe with that person during the years she had been growing up? Her great-aunt might be elderly now, but she was still feisty and fiercely protective of those she loved.

Giselle didn't hesitate. Within seconds of making up her mind she was packing a small case. She was going to flee to Yorkshire.

His second meeting with Hans de Kyper might have produced the kind of result Saul would normally have been celebrating—with Giselle—but right now celebrating anything was the last thing on Saul's mind. It was half an hour since the Dutchman had left, and despite his repeated attempts to ring her he had been unable to make contact with Giselle.

He'd rung, and then texted her on her mobile, and then, when he'd discovered that her mobile phone was switched off, he'd phoned their landline.

Now, when he hadn't been able to get any response from either, he texted Giselle on her Blackberry yet again, asking her to call him, and then he told Moira that he was going home.

Initially when he stepped into the Chelsea house there was nothing to arouse his concern. The cleaners from the concierge service they used had been in. Fresh flowers had been placed in the vases in the hallway and the drawing room, and their bedroom smelled faintly of Giselle's scent—the one he'd had specially blended for her on her birthday. Her laptop was in their shared office, but Giselle herself wasn't. Saul was concerned. It was completely unlike Giselle not to have her phone switched on. He was all too aware of how distressed she was, and now he was beginning to wish that he hadn't left the note for her about the appointment. He had intended his note to be reassuring, but what if Giselle had not interpreted it that way? What if in her current state of mind she had seen it as a threat instead?

Cursing himself under his breath for his earlier lack of awareness, he felt the nagging feeling of concern that had been with him all day flare into urgent and anxious life.

* * *

'Are you all right?'

The kindly female voice pierced through the fog of confusion that had closed Giselle in a wall, distancing her from her surroundings.

'Yes. Yes. Thank you.' She thanked the woman whilst inside a voice screamed like a prisoner battering on a locked and bolted door. *No, no... I am not all right. Please help me.*

Help her? She must help herself. There was no one else to do it. She placed her hand on her flat stomach, nausea making her gag. She was so afraid, so desperately afraid, and so weak. All she wanted was to be with her great-aunt and to seek her advice.

York Station. Giselle felt in the pocket of her luxuriously soft off-white cashmere coat to check that the ticket for the small market town where her great-aunt lived was still there. Just thinking about her great-aunt and her wisdom was helping to calm her. Her great-aunt would understand, she knew.

She wasn't hungry, but she was thirsty, so she bought a bottle of water from one of the station's outlets, thanking the man who served her before huddling deeper into her coat. It was colder up here than it had been in London—or maybe it was just that *she* was colder.

She made her way back to the platform for the Settle train, and took her seat.

It was evening before her taxi finally dropped her off outside the entrance to her great-aunt's retirement home. She'd gone from the station to a hotel and checked in there first, then come straight there. She paused only to exchange a few words with the warden to explain that she had come to see her great-aunt.

The first words her great-aunt said to her once she had greeted her and hugged her were, 'Saul's desperately anxious about you, Giselle. He wants you to get in touch with him.'

'Has he told you about—?' Giselle began.

'About the baby?' her great-aunt interrupted her. 'Yes.' She reached for Giselle's hand and held it tightly between her own. Her skin was paper-thin with age, but her grip was still firm and comforting—just as it had comforted her all those years ago, when she had first gone to live with her. 'We must tell him that you're here. He's very worried.'

Giselle wanted to refuse, but somehow she couldn't find the energy to resist. Just hearing Saul's name on her great-aunt's lips had filled her with such a great need to see him and be held by him, and with it came the deepest kind of sorrow—because she knew she must deny her love for him.

'Very well,' she agreed, nodding her head, her mouth dry as she reached inside her handbag for her Blackberry. She switched it on, and her heart started racing and then aching as she saw all the calls and texts Saul had sent her. She wasn't strong enough to speak personally to him. She knew that she would break down if she did, and beg him for what he would not want to give her. Instead she texted him, telling him that she was with her great-aunt and that he was not to worry any more, before quickly switching off the phone again. She hoped that Saul would not take it into his head to come up here after her. But even if he did it would be morning before he could get here, and by then hopefully she would be feeling more composed and would have her arguments all in place.

'Saul wants me to see this professor,' she told her great-aunt. 'He is an expert on the subject of postnatal depression. Saul feels that the professor should be the one to advise us about…about what decision we should make, but I've already made up my mind. I love my baby so much already.'

Was that sympathy or sadness she could see in her great-aunt's eyes? Was her great-aunt going to let her down after all and side with Saul? Tension gripped Giselle's muscles.

'Giselle my dear, there is something I must say to you,' her great-aunt announced firmly. "And that is that whilst I understand how you feel with regard to your mother's mental illness, it does not necessarily follow that you will be the same. I tried to tell you this whilst you were growing up, but the effects of the trauma you experienced were such that I never felt you were able to hear what I was saying. The truth is,' she told Giselle bracingly, 'I have always felt that you are very much more like the Freeman side of the family—like my mother and your great-grandmother on your father's side. I see so much of my own mother in you, Giselle. I always have done. You have her looks, her colouring, and her courage.'

Relief and gratitude flooded through Giselle. Her great-aunt was trying to make her feel better, but it was true that in looks Giselle was nothing like her own mother, who had been dark-haired and brown-eyed. Even the shape of Giselle's face and the features on it very different from her mother's. Her mannerisms and tone of voice were much more in line with those of her great-aunt, Giselle knew, but then it was her great-aunt who had brought her up and nurtured her.

Much as she wanted to believe what her great-aunt said, Giselle still shook her head and told her, 'It doesn't matter what I say. Saul is determined that I have to see this professor. I don't want to, though.'

'Giselle, my dear, I do understand how you feel. But don't you think that you might be being unfair to Saul?'

'Because I don't want to see the professor? But I'm so frightened of what he might tell me.' Giselle spread her hands in a gesture of defeat and a plea for understanding.

It was gone nine o'clock so, knowing that the residents of the retirement home tended to go to bed early, Giselle told her great-aunt that she would ask the warden to ring for a taxi for her.

'You can't go yet,' her great-aunt protested, looking unusually agitated as she glanced towards the entrance door of her small bedsit. 'Why don't you stay a bit longer and have supper with me? You must be hungry.'

Hungry? Was she? Food was the last thing she had thought about today, but her great-aunt was insisting, and becoming even more agitated at the thought of Giselle leaving without having something to eat, so Giselle felt obliged to give in and agree that, yes, some supper would be lovely.

Although the retirement home provided round-the-clock, twenty-four-hour service for those who lived there, Giselle was struggling to stifle her yawns by the time a young girl arrived, pushing a trolley on which was a pot of tea and some sandwiches. The sight of them unexpectedly set her tummy rumbling.

Half an hour later, encouraged by her great-aunt to eat the last of the sandwiches and have a second cup of tea, she was protesting that she couldn't possibly keep her elderly relative up any longer when the sound of a helicopter close at hand reverberated through the late evening silence.

'What on earth—?' Giselle began, but her great-aunt interrupted her immediately.

'Oh, that will be Sir John Haycroft. It's his new toy, and he's forever flying all over the place in it.'

Giselle nodded her head, stifling another yawn, oblivious to her great-aunt's anxious glances towards the door of her small apartment. The sudden ring on the bell made Giselle jump a little, and then tell her aunt ruefully, 'That will be the warden, coming to say that I've outstayed my welcome. I'll go and tell her that I'm leaving.'

Only when Giselle opened the door it wasn't the warden standing there, it was Saul—and Saul as she had never seen him before. Saul looked as though he had aged a decade. He was in need of a shave and, ridiculously, looked not only as though he had aged during the twenty four hours since she had last see him but also as though he had grown thinner.

As she stepped back into the room Giselle cast a look

at her great-aunt, who was looking flushed but determined as she told Saul triumphantly, 'I did what you asked, Saul, and kept her here. Although it was touch and go.'

Watching her husband hug her great-aunt, and seeing the genuine affection between them, Giselle felt her heart ache anew. When a relationship ended it wasn't just the two people most intimately concerned who were affected. The ripples from the break-up spread and affected others as well.

'I've come to take you home,' was all Saul said to her, but he was looking at her in a way that made her heart turn over in a mixture of intense love and raw agony. 'We need to talk—about everything.'

Her aunt broke in unexpectedly to ask Giselle directly, 'You want this baby, don't you, Giselle?'

The directness of the question undermined Giselle's defences.

'Yes,' she admitted. 'I do. The creation of a new life is such a special thing.' Her voice dropped to a whisper. 'A gift, a privilege. My baby—our baby—has the right to live.' She took a deep breath and lifted her head to look at them both, but especially Saul. 'I *will* see the professor, but I've decided that…that I want our child to be born—even if it means that for its own safety and happiness another woman has to bring it up. I'd rather that than risk hurting it.'

Giselle wasn't sure how she had come to this painful decision, she only knew that having come to it she now felt an overwhelming sense of peace, a sense of having given her baby safety and security by the best means she could.

'Giselle!' Saul protested, stunned by the stark reality of what her words had revealed to him.

But she simply shook her head. 'It's the right thing to do,' she told him tiredly. 'I love you, Saul, but I love our baby too. I am going to have our baby, and nothing you can say will make me change my mind.'

'I don't want you to change your mind.'

Giselle stared at him, convinced she must have misheard.

'Go with him, Giselle,' her great-aunt was begging.

The energy to resist them was seeping relentlessly from her, and as though she was being propelled by a force greater than she was herself she found that she was walking towards Saul. Because she wanted to be with him, Giselle admitted to herself weakly. She ached and longed to be with him. She wanted the strength of his arms around her, the comfort of his shoulder to lean on, the love she knew he had for her to support her.

Tiredly she gave in to her own weak longings and nodded her head, kissing her great-aunt on the cheek before going to Saul's side.

'I'll have to cancel my room at the hotel,' she murmured.

'Already done,' Saul told her, making it plain that he hadn't intended to return to London without her. 'Come on, the chopper pilot's waiting. I'd have hired a helicopter and flown it myself for you, but I didn't dare trust myself to concentrate on flying and not worrying about you.'

As she listened to Saul guilt filled Giselle, but she

didn't say anything. How could she? Whichever decision she had made someone would have suffered, and she knew she would always feel guilty about the decision she had chosen to make. How could she not?

Once they were inside the helicopter, with Saul sitting up-front with the pilot and acting as co-pilot, there was no real opportunity for them to talk privately. And Giselle felt so exhausted and drained by the events of the day that she was practically asleep by the time they landed at City Airport.

From there it was only a short taxi ride to their Chelsea house. The hallway was filled with the scent of the morning's new delivery of lilies and the brilliant light from the chandeliers—so carefully chosen by Giselle because they'd been made at a start-up factory in Poland, which trained and employed young apprentices who had previously been out of work. The light illuminated the just off-white paint she had spent such a long time choosing, to make sure that its grey-blue undertone added just a hint of colour to the hallway that she felt chimed with the colour of Chelsea's sky and river backdrop. But tonight the atmosphere of lived-in elegance and comfort reflected by her interior design choices failed to have its normal restorative effect on Giselle's senses.

'You look dead on your feet.' Saul told her. 'Go and get ready for bed, and I'll make us both a drink and bring it up.'

Much as she longed for a warm bath, Giselle had to make do with a shower, half afraid that she was so tired she might actually fall asleep in the bath. She was exhausted really, but she desperately needed to understand if Saul had actually meant what he had said at her great-aunt's about wanting their baby.

Saul came into the bedroom just as she emerged from the bathroom, wrapped in a thick towelling robe.

'Cocoa?' she exclaimed in astonishment, as she saw the milky drinks he had made.

'They always used to make it for us at my boarding school if we were feeling low,' Saul told her simply.

'I didn't know we had any in the house.'

'We didn't. I bought it this afternoon.' He placed the mugs on his bedside table and turned to face her. 'Giselle, you can't mean what you said about giving up our baby for someone else to raise.'

'I do mean it,' she assured him. 'At least that way it will have life, and…and safety.'

'And its mother's love?' Saul demanded fiercely.

Giselle's whole body shook. She knew how Saul felt about a child's need for its mother's love, because he had been denied that. 'I shall always love our child. But for its sake…'

'We are going to see the professor, Giselle, and I won't take no for an answer. You will be a wonderful mother, and I can't allow you to even think of depriving our child of its mother's love and presence in its life.'

'It will have you—if you meant what you said at my great-aunt's?' Giselle trembled as she phrased her words as a question.

'I did.' Saul's voice was firm. 'I shall be there for our child, Giselle, and I promise so will you.'

'I'd love to believe that, but I dare not let myself. I want our baby so much, Saul.'

'That makes two of us.' Saul's smile was slightly slanted and wry. 'I don't know how it happened myself, Giselle, but all I've been able to think of since you told me was you saying how much you'd have wanted our children, my children, had things been different. Gradually, almost without me knowing it, as the baby has grown inside you, so a protective love for it has grown inside *me*. I felt such a tug of fiercely paternal love inside me that it stunned me, robbing me of the ability to say or do anything. I was shocked, I admit it. That was why I didn't say anything to you there and then. How I felt was so totally contrary to everything I'd always thought I would feel if I allowed myself to imagine our child. The resentment, the jealousy, the fear of losing you I'd suspected I'd see in myself just weren't there. I was in a daze.

'I should have told you. I wanted to. But I was afraid that if I did it would put even more pressure on you, and that you'd be even more afraid of being like your mother. That's why I want you to see the professor—so that he can reassure you and tell you what I already know. You will be a wonderful mother.'

Hope, belief, joy, life. Like stars glimmering in a dark night sky, the words lit up in Giselle's mind until the light from them and from her own relief dazzled her.

'You've changed your mind? You want our baby?' Giselle's words were soft with all that she felt for this most wonderful of men—a man strong enough to show his weakness to her, strong enough, too, to allow the course he had chosen for his life to be diverted for the sake of the tiny spark of life they had ignited together.

Saul nodded his head.

'Don't ask me how it happened, because I don't have an answer. I only know that inside my head I have an image of the two of you together that does things to me I thought impossible.'

'Oh, Saul, you don't know how much this means to me—knowing that you will be there for our baby even if I can't be. Knowing that he or she will grow up with you to love them and protect them.'

'Don't speak like that, Giselle—as though you aren't going to be part of that. Because you are.'

'You can't say that. We don't know that. No matter how much I want it to be so. But I feel so much better now, Saul, so much stronger. Knowing that our baby will have your love gives me that strength. I *will* see the professor now, and we can tell him that no matter what happens to…to me, you will always be there for our child. That's if he will see me after I didn't keep the appointment you made.'

'He will see you. I've already spoken to him, and he said to tell you that he perfectly understands how you feel. We will *both* be there for our child, Giselle. I know it.' Saul's voice was raw with emotion.

He reached for her hand and held it whilst they looked at one another.

'We'll find a way through this, Giselle. We'll find a way to make it work—and there *will* be a way. What happened with your mother was appalling and tragic, and I can't begin to imagine the trauma you must have gone through—a six-year-old having to cope with something like that without help.'

'I had my great-aunt,' Giselle reminded him gently. 'She was wonderful. She explained everything to me as I got old enough to understand.'

'But her explanations didn't stop your fears, or the grief you felt inside yourself, did they?' Saul challenged her, equally gently. 'They didn't stop you feeling guilty even though you should have been the last one in the whole situation to feel that.' His hand tightened over hers. 'You have no need to be anything other than what you are,' he assured her fiercely. 'You are everything you should and could be already. You are the wheel on which my life turns, Giselle, the heart of everything I do. I promise you that somehow we will find a way to set you free from your fear. Medical science has improved dramatically since your mother gave birth.'

'So you keep saying. But postnatal depression still strikes down many, many mothers. I've seen it on the internet. I've read stories of those women who have suffered from it.' When Saul shook his head she said, 'Yes, I know it might have been better for me to avoid reading them, but I had to, Saul. I had to know.'

She had read so many heart-rending stories from mothers who had suffered postnatal depression. And read many too from mothers who had overcome it, with medical and family help.

'My mother's depression was more a psychosis. I found out from my great-aunt that my father was told she should have been sectioned, but he had refused— both out of love for her and out of fear for the effect it could have on his patients if it became known that he couldn't cure his own wife.'

'Well, I promise you this, Giselle. I intend to fight as hard now for you to have our child as I would once have done to prevent its conception. As I have discovered, the reality of a conceived child is very different from the concept of a child that only exists inside one's head. The truth is that neither of us can reject the life we have created. We are already connected to it and it to us by the strongest of human ties. It is part of us and we are part of it.'

'Oh, Saul,' Giselle whispered as he took her in his arms and held her tightly. 'If there is such a thing as a guardian angel then mine must have been watching over me today. I am so grateful, so lucky, so truly blessed. How did you know I'd gone to my great-aunt's?'

'Where else would you go? I couldn't raise you on your phone, and you didn't come home. I guessed that you'd head for Yorkshire and your great-aunt, so I telephoned her and she agreed that she'd let me know if you turned up. She rang me whilst you were talking to the warden, who'd alerted her to your arrival. Here.' Saul released her to pick up one of the mugs and hand it to her. 'Drink this before it goes cold. It will be all right, Giselle,' he assured her, his voice full of certainty. 'I promise you that it will.'

CHAPTER ELEVEN

'WE WILL FIND A WAY,' Saul had promised her just over six months ago. And he had certainly done everything any person could be expected to do and more to find that way, Giselle acknowledged.

There had been consultations, examinations, discussions, research, and further consultations. At the end of them, the eminent expert in the field of postnatal depression, Professor Edward Green—whose manner had melted away the last of Giselle's fears for their baby the minute he had shaken her hand and she had seen the compassion and understanding in his eyes—had devised what he and Saul both considered to be a foolproof programme of care for Giselle and her baby. They had both reassured her it would make it impossible for even the slightest symptom of postnatal depression not to be noticed and dealt with promptly.

Their son—for the baby she was carrying was a boy—would be delivered by Caesarean section in five weeks' time, at full term—Professor Green did not hold with the fashion for mothers to want their sections performed early for the sake of their figures—and from that moment onwards, whilst she was in the expensive private maternity hospital in London and afterwards when she went home to the Chelsea house, she would have a live-in specially trained nurse on hand to monitor the situation for as long as she and Saul and the professor deemed it necessary.

She was indeed, Giselle believed, truly blessed to have such a loving husband, to be carrying a healthy baby, and to have the medical care of such an understanding and compassionate expert.

Although Giselle wanted to look after their baby herself, she had agreed that it made sense to have a nanny as well as her own special nurse. In fact if she was honest, she admitted, she had been a little afraid of refusing in case either the professor or Saul thought that her refusal might indicate a burgeoning hormonal problem within her even before she gave birth.

Giselle put down the clothes she had been packing ahead of their departure for a brief three-day visit to Arezzio, for Saul's coronation. Saul had told her that he would understand if she preferred to stay in London, but she had insisted that she wanted to be with him—which she did.

The trouble was that Saul, being Saul, had now immersed himself so completely in every aspect of postnatal depression that Giselle sometimes felt as though Saul and Professor Edwards were on one side of a fence watching her, whilst she was on the other on her own. She had seen the expression of concern on Saul's face when she had told him that she would prefer not to have a nanny and instantly had felt anxious and wary, unwilling to tell him about her intensely powerful surge of maternal possessiveness over the child that was growing within her. *She* wanted to be the one to care for their son. *She* wanted to hold him and bathe him, to mother him in all respects, instead of simply being allowed to feed him.

In the early stages of their discussions with the professor, when Giselle had asked him what would happen if she *did* develop severe postnatal depression, he had told her that the very worst-case scenario would be that she would be hospitalised for treatment, and that if things did come to that he would arrange for the baby's nanny to have a room at the private clinic where she would be treated, so that Giselle could continue to see her baby under supervision— 'So the baby's bond with you isn't prejudiced.'

She had been relieved, of course, to know that no matter what her child would be safe, but at the same time the closer she got to full term the more anxious she became that she might inadvertently do something that would signal to the two men watching over her that she wasn't fit to look after her own child. Giselle didn't think she could bear that.

As her baby had grown inside the safe protection of her womb, so her love for it had grown, and now she felt as fiercely protective and possessive about her baby as a tigress might over its young. Sometimes in her darkest and most lonely moments she even wondered if the depth of her emotional maternal feelings towards her child might not in itself be a sign of something darker— a hint of postnatal depression to come. But that was something she couldn't discuss with anyone—least of all Saul, who had turned into the kind of father-to-be that she suspected most woman would want. He was tender and loving towards her, putting the needs of her pregnancy to the forefront of everything he did. Because of the number of consultations they had had with the professor, and his advice that the baby should be delivered in England, Saul had even insisted they stay on in the London house and he would work from there.

And that had been another problem. She had had to fight very hard indeed to get Saul to accept that she was perfectly healthy enough to work, and even harder to make him understand that she actually *needed* to work. In fact her pregnancy had made her even more anxious to press on with their plans for those in need. Reluctantly Saul had given way.

At least he had agreed that she could continue to travel with him, so she had been able to witness the preparations for his coronation, which had been timed to take place in the same month as his long-ago ancestors had first ascended the throne.

Giselle smiled ruefully to herself. She knew she would never forget the expression on Saul's face when they had first been told that their baby was a boy. Whilst her own feeling had been one of relief that at least this child would be spared the genetic inheritance she feared, Saul's expression had said all Giselle needed to know about men and their pride in creating sons.

'I meant what I said about the country becoming a democracy,' Saul had told her that evening.

'Good,' Giselle had responded truthfully.

'The business will be there for our son if he wants to

go into it, just as there will be a place for him as Head
of State if he wants that. But he will not be the country's
absolute ruler.'

'Neither of us would want that for him,' Giselle had
agreed. 'That kind of inheritance can be as much of a
burden as it is a benefit.'

'I want him to grow up to be his own man—to form
his own opinions and to be...'

'Like you?' Giselle had suggested mischievously.

They had made love that night, Saul tender and careful, and everything he felt for her and their coming child
had been there in his touch and his words of love to
her.

Now, though, sometimes in her most anxious and
despairing moments, she wondered if he loved the child
she was carrying more than he did her.

She had seen both the professor and her obstetrician and midwife yesterday, to check that she was all
right to fly now that she was eight months pregnant, and
they had reassured her that everything was perfectly in
order.

Giselle had been pleased about that. She desperately wanted to see Saul crowned, and to be there for
him on such an important once-in-a-lifetime occasion.
Becoming the ruler of the country might not be what
he had wanted—he wasn't one for pomp and ceremony—but she knew that as soon as he could he would
start gently but firmly steering the country towards
democracy.

Saul himself came into the bedroom just as she was

about to close her suitcase, frowning when he saw what she was doing.

'You should have left that for me to do,' he told her. 'These next few days are going to be tiring enough for you as it is.'

'I'm having a baby, Saul. I'm not an invalid,' she reminded him. The maternity outfit she was wearing—soft stretchy layers of fine cashmere in shades of caramel and cream—would be perfect beneath her cashmere coat. Now, although it was April, there was still a definite bite in the air, despite the sunshine they had been having.

'You don't have to come, you know,' Saul told her. 'I'll only be gone three days.'

'Four, including tonight—and besides, I want to come,' Giselle said, adding with a smile, 'We both do. I can assure you that your son has been very good today—only half a dozen somersaults and a few kicks since I told him if he was overactive he wouldn't be able to be there when his daddy is crowned.'

'He won't know what's happening!' Saul laughed.

'He'll know something's happening,' Giselle insisted. 'He'll be able to sense it and feel it. I *want* to be there, Saul.' Her voice grew more serious. 'When the Archbishop puts that crown on your head I know you will be thinking of Aldo, and all that could have been for him. It will be such a solemn and sacred moment— the final moment, perhaps, that you will feel him close to you.'

Saul turned to her and put his hands on her shoulders. 'How is it that you always manage to vocalise exactly what I'm feeling when I can't even formulate or make sense of those feelings myself?'

'I'm a woman,' Giselle told him. 'We're good at those things.'

CHAPTER TWELVE

IT WAS ALMOST MIDNIGHT when they finally let themselves into their apartments in the palace, and Giselle admitted to herself, although she wasn't prepared to admit it to Saul, that she felt very tired indeed.

Saul, though, was obviously more percipient than she had thought, because once they were in bed, her head resting on his shoulder, he told her quietly, 'I know you've arranged to drive over and see how things are progressing with the plans for the rebuilding work in the mining town, but I think we should cancel it. I don't want you overdoing things.'

'It's a two-hour drive, Saul, that's all. And all I shall be doing is sitting in the car and then walking a few yards.'

'We'll see,' was all Saul would say.

Once Giselle's even breathing told him that she was asleep he leaned back against his pillow in the darkness, contemplating the dramatic changes that fate had brought him. In his wallet, and normally close to his heart, was the first scan image they had seen of their baby—their son—and with it was a photograph of Giselle. As he closed his eyes his final thoughts of the day were as they were every day now—of his hope that Giselle would not suffer from the postnatal depression she feared so much.

'I'd really prefer it if you didn't go, Giselle. You say you slept well last night, but you still look tired, and since I can't come with you because of the meetings I've got to attend, and the run-through for the coronation itself, I wouldn't be happy about you going by yourself.'

'I'm going, and nothing you can say will dissuade me,' Giselle answered Saul as they sat eating their breakfast in their private quarters. The sunshine was bright, but the air outside was still too chilly for them to be able to eat in the courtyard.

Two peacocks had climbed up on top of the wall separating the courtyard from the main lawn of the palace gardens, and their curiosity was making Giselle smile.

'I think we shall have to get a dog. Children need pets,' she mused, laughing when she felt their son kick enthusiastically.

'I always wanted a dog, but my parents wouldn't let me have one because they travelled too much,' said Saul.

A brief knock on the door heralded the arrival of the major-domo, a sheaf of papers under his arm.

'I'll have to go,' Saul told Giselle, kissing her and patting the bulge of her stomach. 'I do wish you'd reconsider visiting the town.'

'Stop worrying. We shall be fine.' She paused, and then told Saul quietly, whilst the major-domo waited discreetly out of earshot, 'I want our son to know how lucky he is, Saul. I want him to know right from the beginning how you and I feel about those in need and about our duty to help them.'

The visit to the mining town had taken up more of the day than Giselle had expected. But, exhausted as she was as she thanked the driver who had escorted her and made her way to their apartments, she was glad that she had gone. Everyone involved in the rebuilding work had been so thrilled to see her, so grateful for everything that she and Saul had done, and so eager to tell her in halting English how happy they were to have Saul as their new ruler.

She had even seen the little girl she had held that day they had first gone there. Plump and smiling now, and dressed in the new clothes she and Saul had provided for all the children, the sight of her had warmed Giselle's heart.

Now, though, she felt so tired that all she wanted to do was lie down and sleep. But Saul would be upset if he realised how exhausted she felt, and, besides, she wanted to hear all about his day. She had taken a lot of photographs of the rebuilding work to store on her laptop, and she would be able to share them with Saul later, once the coronation was over.

It was disappointing to discover that he wasn't in the apartments. He'd texted her half an hour earlier, to say that he'd almost finished for the day and that he'd organised supper for them both.

Giselle reached round to rub low down in the small of

her back, where an ache had started during the morning drive to the town. The pain had been coming and going on and off ever since, and now was quite severe.

Saul came in just as she was massaging the niggling, aching spot where the pain was seated, and his pointed look caused her to stop and ask him, 'How did the rehearsal go?'

'Very well—well, mostly. They found a worn patch on the cloak, but since it's right at the back no one is going to see it. There's so much gold braid on the official royal uniform that it weights a ton—likewise the crown. I hadn't really seen it close up before, although I attended Aldo's coronation. It's incredibly beautiful, and studded with pearls, diamonds, rubies, emeralds—you name it, they're there. It was made in Florence, apparently, and is no doubt worth a king's ransom, as they say. Likewise the orb and sceptre. I'm trying to persuade them to allow the State jewels to be displayed, so that the people can see them. Far better than sticking them back in some dark vault— What is it?' he demanded, when Giselle made a sudden small sound.

'Nothing,' she assured him. 'Just your son practising his football, or maybe agreeing with your plans.'

She gave Saul a reassuring smile, but the truth was that out of nowhere she had suddenly been seized by a very sharp surge of pain. Not that Saul needed to know that. He would only fuss. After all, she still had another five weeks of her pregnancy left, and everyone had said that it was perfectly safe for her to be here.

Half an hour later, when her waters broke as she stood in the bathroom cleaning her teeth, Giselle knew that it was too late to question the wisdom of that advice. Instead she called out to Saul, gripping the edge of the vanity unit when a fresh surge of pain engulfed her.

'It's the baby,' she told Saul when he came in answer to her call. 'I think—' She broke off, caught up in another wave of pain.

'Stay there. Don't move. I'll get the court physician.'

Moving was the last thing she felt like doing, but Giselle knew that she had to. Saul had only been gone for ten minutes, and in that time she'd had two more pains.

She'd just reached the bedroom when the door burst open, to admit a middle-aged woman with a purposeful look about her.

'I am the court midwife,' she told Giselle in broken English. 'I examine you—if you will allow?'

Behind her, two maids rushed to get the bed ready, whilst Saul dashed off again in search of the doctor, whom he had still not tracked down.

Giselle was helped onto the bed, and the midwife gave her a reassuring smile before saying, 'I go wash. One minute.'

One minute. Her pains were coming every two minutes now, deep and intense, and a very different matter from those pains she had been having earlier.

The midwife returned, but Giselle was barely aware of her presence other than for the reassurance it gave her. She followed the directions of her body and her instincts, and gave herself over to the task of bringing into the world the life that was so fiercely eager to be born.

'Push. You push now.' The midwife's voice reached Giselle through a haze of pain and endurance as she wiped the sweat from Giselle's forehead.

Saul had been banished from the bedroom. Birth plans that included the father's presence at the bedside were apparently something that had not as yet reached the country. Giving birth was women's work, according to the midwife, who had imparted this and a flood of other pieces of wisdom to Giselle as she accompanied her on her journey to give birth.

The effort of pushing had strained and corded the muscles in Giselle's throat. She was so tired, and the pain was so unrelenting. She badly wanted to rest and escape them, but then an urge seized her to make an increased effort, with her whole heart and energy behind the push she gave. There was fresh, seizing pain, and then almost unbelievably a feeling of relief and release and then joy.

The midwife cried triumphantly, 'He is born! Your son!' and then handed the baby to her.

When Saul was finally allowed in, five minutes later, after the midwife had tidied up, Giselle was nursing their son with a look on her face of such transparent shimmering joy and love that Saul had to blink away his own tears at just watching them together.

They had already chosen a name for him—Lucas— and now, seeing Saul standing at the side of the bed, Giselle held the baby up to him and said softly, 'Lucas, say hello to your daddy. He's the image of you, Saul,' she added emotionally. 'He has your eyes and your nose. He is exactly like you.'

Saul wasn't going to disagree. He was already as besotted with the small scrap of humanity he was holding in his arms as Giselle.

It was only later, when mother and baby were both asleep, resting after their shared act of birth, that Saul recognised the situation they were now in. Giselle had given birth. She and their son were safe and well. For now. But if she should develop postnatal depression, what then? All the safeguards they had put in place were in London. Giselle and the baby were here.

The coronation would have to be cancelled, Saul decided. Giselle was far more important to him. Her welfare came first.

'Cancel the coronation?' Shock filled her. 'But you can't possibly do that,' Giselle protested to Saul. She had just finished feeding Lucas, and had handed him to Saul to put in the cot beside their bed. 'If you want to know what I think, it's that your son was in such a hurry to be born because he wants to be there for it,' she insisted.

Saul gave her an indulgent look, but then said practically, 'We have to get back to London, and the sooner the better. I don't want to delay our return any longer than necessary. I've already spoken to the professor, and he agrees with me that it makes sense to get you back to London asap.'

'Because neither of you trust me with Lucas?' The accusation was out before Giselle could stop herself.

'Of course I trust you with him,' Saul insisted. 'It's you I'm concerned about, Giselle. You've said all along how much safer you feel with everything we've put in place.'

That was true, but what she hadn't said to him was how imprisoned by those safeguards she had begun to feel. And that feeling had been increased tenfold by Lucas's birth. Now all she wanted was to be alone with her baby and Saul. The thought of having to share Lucas's care with anyone else set her heart sinking, and made her want to reach for her baby and hold him tightly.

'I don't want to go back, Saul. Not yet. Not before your coronation,' Giselle insisted. 'Three more days aren't going to make very much difference. Ask the professor if you don't believe me—or if you feel you can't trust me with Lucas.'

Saul tried to soothe her. 'Of course I can trust you with him.'

Giselle gave him an apologetic look. 'I'm sorry. It's just…' How could she tell him that his words had taken from her some of the joy she had felt in Lucas's birth, reminding her of what she did not want to think about? Not now, in these precious first hours of their son's life.

Twenty-four hours later Saul's coronation took place, with Giselle sitting watching, Lucas in her arms, and a discreetly concealed buggy tucked close at hand. Saul looked magnificent, as she had known he would, and his speech to his people after the coronation, broadcast on the country's television network and to those who had gathered in the square below the palace steps, made her eyes prickle with suppressed tears of pride in her husband.

She hadn't missed the special private look Saul had given her and Lucas when he spoke about the importance of family life and the need for the country to work together as a family.

As soon as the formalities were over she was going to retreat to their apartments, leaving Saul to do the meeting and greeting and mixing with people whilst she rested—as the midwife had insisted that she must.

Although all the baby books she'd read had warned that three days or so after the birth she might expect to be hit by tears and the baby blues, and that this was quite natural and nothing to worry about, Giselle was relieved that it didn't seem to be the case for her. Lucas was the most wonderful baby—strong and not too demanding, sleeping and feeding well—but he was already showing a strength of character that delighted them both.

Once she'd fed and changed Lucas, she put him down for his nap. They'd turned her dressing room into a temporary nursery, and Giselle left the door open when she went back to the bedroom for a rest herself, so that she would hear him if he woke up and cried for her.

Giselle looked as though she was still asleep, lying in bed with her eyes closed, when Saul walked into the bedroom two hours later, frowning as he listened to the professor, who had telephoned him.

'Yes, of course I'm keeping a close eye on things,

and on Giselle,' he confirmed to the other man. 'She is very emotional, as I've already told you.'

In the bed, where she had simply been lying with her eyes closed, thinking how lucky she was, Giselle tensed with apprehension. Saul was watching her, he had said. Because he didn't trust her with their son. Giselle knew that the intensity of the pain that caused her was illogical, but her sense of separation from Saul, the feeling that she couldn't talk to him openly and honestly about how she felt for fear of him thinking that what she said might be a sign of incipient postnatal depression, was making her feel defensive and very alone—as though Saul was no longer on her side.

Oddly, her own fear that she might harm her baby had disappeared the moment she had first held Lucas in her arms. She had known it instinctively and immediately, but of course other people couldn't be expected to understand or trust in that. Other people like the professor— but surely not Saul as well? Surely *he* should be able to sense what she felt and believe in it?

Two days later they were back in London, where Giselle managed just over two weeks of what felt like having her every minute with Lucas and her every breath monitored by the professor's nurse, whilst she had to watch the nanny taking over what she felt was *her* rightful role as Lucas's mother, before she finally snapped. She turned on Saul one evening after they'd had dinner together and he was asking her solicitously how she felt.

'You don't *care* how I feel,' she accused him angrily. 'No one does. I'm sick of being watched all the time, of having twice-daily discussions with the nurse about my feelings, so that she can report them to the professor—as though I'm on probation as a mother. I can't even take Lucas out in his buggy without either the nurse or the nanny fussing and looking at me as though they don't trust me. I want them both to leave.'

She waited for Saul to protest, to warn her to remember why they were there, but instead to her astonishment he simply said, 'Good.'

'Good?' Giselle repeated.

'Yes, good,' Saul agreed. 'When I told the professor that in my view you are perfectly mentally and emotionally stable he agreed with me. But he said there was no point in telling you that, and that you would have to reach that conclusion yourself before we could remove from you the props that neither of us believe you need.'

'Reach that conclusion myself? I knew the minute Lucas was *born* that I would be all right. *You* were the one who insisted on bringing me back here like a…a prisoner. *You* were the one who didn't trust me.'

'Not trust you? Of course I trusted you. Like you, I knew the first second I saw you with Lucas that you would never hurt him.'

They looked at one another for a minute, and then Giselle told him shakily, 'I've felt so alone, Saul. As though we've been on different sides of something. I've missed you so much.'

'I just wanted to hold back and give you time to make up your own mind about what was right for you.'

They both started to laugh.

* * *

Six weeks later, when both the professor and Giselle's obstetrician pronounced her well and healthy, Giselle and Saul celebrated the news in one another's arms— whilst their son, very thoughtfully, remained happily and contentedly asleep.

EPILOGUE

'YOU SEE—I TOLD YOU that you are a Freeman, and nothing like your mother,' Giselle's great-aunt announced six months later, as she stood proudly holding her great-great-nephew outside Arezzio's cathedral for a formal christening photograph.

Giselle laughed, unable to resist smiling down into her son's face as he held out his hand to her. It seemed impossible now to imagine that she had ever thought she might harm her own child, or suffer from the same devastating illness that had struck down her mother. Motherhood for her was the crowning jewel in her happiness—a true joy and delight that had enriched the love she and Saul shared and fulfilled her. Although she hadn't as yet said anything to Saul, she was already thinking about increasing their family.

'What's that smile for?' Saul asked her, detaching himself from the group of ministers surrounding him to come over to her.

'Oh, nothing,' Giselle told him.

Saul leaned forward and said softly, 'This *nothing* wouldn't have anything to do with any plans on your part that might involve increasing the size of the nursery, would it?'

'Saul! How did you guess—?' She broke off, and then laughed at herself for giving the game away.

Her laughter was silenced by Saul's brief but fiercely passionate kiss.

'I know you, and I love you, which is why I knew all along that our son would have the best mother in the world.'

She was so lucky. So incredibly, wonderfully, blessed and lucky. And she knew it. She would never cease giving thanks for all that she had. She would never stop counting her blessings.

Harlequin *Presents*

Coming Next Month

from **Harlequin Presents® EXTRA.** Available February 8, 2011.

Coming Next Month

from **Harlequin Presents®.** Available February 22, 2011.

JEMIMA yanked open a drawer in the sideboard to find Alfie's birth certificate. Her son was her husband's child. It was a question of telling the truth whether she liked it or not. She extended the certificate to Alejandro.

"This has to be nonsense," Alejandro asserted.

"Well, if you can find some other way of explaining how I managed to give birth by that date and Alfie not be yours, I'd like to hear it," Jemima challenged.

Alejandro glanced up, golden eyes bright as blades and as dangerous. "All this proves is that you must still have been pregnant when you walked out on our marriage. It does not automatically follow that the child is mine."

"'I know it doesn't suit you to hear this news now and I really didn't want to tell you. But I can't lie to you about it. Someday Alfie may want to look you up and get acquainted."

"If what you have just told me is the truth, if that little boy does prove to be mine, it was vindictive and extremely selfish of you to leave me in ignorance!"

Jemima paled. "When I left you, I had no idea that I was still pregnant."

"Two years is a long period of time, yet you made no attempt to inform me that I might be a father. I will want DNA tests to confirm your claim before I make any decision about what I want to do."

"Do as you like," she told him curtly. "*I* know who Alfie's father is and there has never been any doubt of his identity."

"I will make arrangements for the tests to be carried out and I will see you again when the result is available," Alejandro drawled with lashings of dark Spanish masculine reserve.

"I'll contact a solicitor and start the divorce," Jemima proffered in turn.

Alejandro's eyes narrowed in a piercing scrutiny that made her uncomfortable. "It would be foolish to do anything before we have that DNA result."

"I disagree," Jemima flashed back. "I should have applied for a divorce the minute I left you!"

Alejandro quirked an ebony brow. "And why didn't you?"

Jemima dealt him a fulminating glance but said nothing, merely moving past him to open her front door in a blunt invitation for him to leave.

"I'll be in touch," he delivered on the doorstep.

What is Alejandro's next move? Perhaps rekindling their marriage is the only solution! But will Jemima agree?

Find out in Lynne Graham's
exciting new romance
JEMIMA'S SECRET

Available March 2011
from Harlequin Presents®.